CONTACT
OF THE
BEST KIND

CONTACT
OF THE
BEST KIND

2ND EDITION: FRIENDSHIP

G. G. ROYAL

Contact of the Best Kind 2nd Edition: Friendship by G. G. Royal

This book is written to provide information and motivation to readers. Its purpose is not to render any type of psychological, legal, or professional advice of any kind. The content is the sole opinion and expression of the author, and not necessarily that of the publisher.

Printed in the United States of America.

ISBN 978-1-955363-72-3 (Paperback)
ISBN 978-1-955363-73-0 (Digital)

Lettra Press books may be ordered through booksellers or by contacting:

Lettra Press LLC
30 N Gould St. Suite 4753
Sheridan, WY 828011
1 307-200-3414 | info@lettrapress.com
www.lettrapress.com

Contact of the Best Kind 2nd Edition: Friendship

by G. G. Royal
Lettra Press

book review by Jennifer Hummer

"Whose story do you think is easier to believe? That I saw a 100 foot long sea monster or that you saw aliens?"

Royal has created an intriguing story, filled with daring rescues and high-stakes drama. By incorporating mysterious real-life events into his narrative, he adds another layer of intrigue to his readers. The connection between the controversial alien ship crash in Roswell in 1947 and the strange happenings around the Bermuda Triangle form a clever plotline. Although these events are still officially unproven, it's delightfully plausible that a child born from aliens who crash-landed at Roswell would be stuck living on earth.

When they discover each other, Abby and Michael could have let fear take over, but instead, they work together to come up with their rescue plan. The dialogue is well written, and Royal creates an abundance of interwoven storylines throughout the novel. Overall, this is a unique story, and the author has taken great care in developing his characters to fit a very creative plotline.

CHAPTER ONE

On the Georgia coast a plastic Coke bottle bobs up and immediately succumbs to the swift incoming tide and current that carries it into the mouth of Fancy Bluff Creek. It floats along passing docks and houses as water fills the creeks of the Golden Isle's marshlands. All the fiddler crabs retreat into their muddy holes until the tide goes out again. Soon the marsh will be underwater and only the top of the bright green sawgrass will be visible.

Levi Benjamin stood observing the incoming tide on the end of the long wooden dock behind his home where he lived with his dad, Dan. He was about to cast his net to catch a few shrimp while the tide was coming in. There was a short time span for catching shrimp and his dad asked him to catch enough for dinner. First he wanted to check his crab baskets. He pulled the first of his two crab baskets up and it had six aggressive blue crabs in it. They had bright blue tips on the ends of their evil-looking oversized claws and they were backed into the corners, clicking their claws together at him to keep him away. He threw the basket back in and lifted the other which had four blue crabs in it. A couple of them were too small and dad would throw those and the females back in. He threw it back and picked up his net to prepare to cast. His net was a little large for him but he could throw it. He slipped the loop at the end of the casting net rope over his right wrist then he deftly looped the remaining rope like a lasso and held it in his right hand. He picked up and held the net high by the middle holding everything in his right hand. He stuck out his right hand forefinger and looped a small section of the weighted edge of the net hanging down over his forefinger. He finally reached 2 or 3 feet down with his left hand and lifted the edge up and out so he could hold and spread out the net as much of it as he could to get it to open. Then he twisted his upper body like he was holding a giant floppy Frisbee and using his whole upper body as if it were a coiled spring, he spun around, tossing the net out and watching as it began to unfurl out over the top of the water. Sometimes it worked better than other times. He knew practice makes perfect when it comes to casting a net.

His solid black cat, Blackie, was eagerly waiting to pounce on whatever he pulled out, whether it was a shrimp or fish, Blackie always got his share first. The few shrimp Levi did catch with each cast was put in an ice chest with water and a lid on it. They would jump right out of the ice chest if it wasn't closed.

He was about ready to go inside when he spotted a plastic Coke bottle floating, bobbing and being carried along by the current toward his dock. He always removed any trash he could in his part of the creek and he thought he might be able to catch this bottle with his net as it came by. He watched it as it came closer, edging down the river, caught up in a little tidal whirlpool. It stayed in the current and kept coming closer. He picked his net up and prepared to cast it. He put a little of the edge between his extended arms, into his mouth to take up slack and to get a longer reach. As the bottle drifted closer and was about to come into range, he twisted his upper body and whipped the net around in a wide arch. "Perfect shot," he told Blackie. He let the weighted circular ring around the outer edge of the net settle for a few seconds over the bottle and then began pulling it in by the line that threaded all the way around the outer edge and up through the middle with a slip knot that allowed him to close the net as he was pulling it in, capturing whatever was within its grasp like a cuttlefish. For a second it felt like the net was getting caught on something big but with a little tug it was loose.

He guessed it was either a good-sized fish or maybe it was just the tide whipping it around.

He and Blackie came down here a lot. He liked fishing, shrimping and crabbing and he could do all three at the same time off his own personal dock. He took pride in keeping the area around it clean by pulling old trash out of the water when he saw it. Trash would get caught in the tall sawgrass in the marshes around here and Levi thought it looked disgusting. Old bags and cups he could usually catch with his net or he would use his reel to hook them. This was his part of the river so he always removed anything plastic he saw floating in the water. He knew how important it was to keep the area clean because he and others around here ate the seafood from this river. His dad caught a black drum fish in his shrimp net not long after they bought it. It weighed about 50 pounds. Dad said he got 26 fillets out of that fish. He called the neighbor's and had a Labor Day feast made just from the seafood caught from this creek. Dad was excited that he could pull off a neighborhood feast that everyone loved with food caught from his dock. That was one of the reasons he had said they moved here.

Levi liked coming out here in the evenings. He would sit on the dock and watch his fishing line as the sun set. He was transfixed by all the colors of the evening sky and he would come in only when it got too dark to see. Dad pointed out to him once that he should pay attention to how spectacular the sunsets could be here. He knew it was refracted light as the sun sets on the western horizon, he had learned a little about it in school. The clouds made every night different though, with all their different designs and colors, you have to see it to appreciate it. Sometimes they were spectacular. Now, he hardly ever misses one. He even hurries out to the dock some evenings just to see what it looks like. He also loved watching the long legged sea birds coming and going oblivious to his presence. He loved watching Pink Roseate Spoonbills combing the water for shrimp and small fish while Great White Egrets and Tri-colored Herons fished along the shallow edges. He has seen dolphins and otters swimming past at near high tide and maybe even a small whale once. He liked casting his net to see if he could catch an unsuspecting fish or something else passing by. You just never know what you'll catch. The tide brings the entire river by his dock twice a day. And every sunset was different because every day was new. In Levi's mind was always the hope that he might catch something big in the next toss.

He was optimistic because his dad was. He had a love of investigating lots of interesting things. Dad explained that he should meet every sunset as new because you will never see it or an identical one again. Then, he would continue on to some point he wanted to make, just like every sunset is different and beautiful, every person is different and beautiful, which is why we must treat each other with kindness and respect. "Besides," he would say, "it takes a long time to really get to know most people so while you're getting to know someone, good manners are a universal language," or something like that.

They would sit out here together, spraying insect repellent on each other as the no-see-ums and mosquitoes swarmed the night skies. On clear nights, stars filled the sky. Dad liked pointing out constellations. He knew a lot about them. He said he had read a novel called "Space" by Michener as a kid and became interested then. He even made up a riddle. He asked, "If the sun goes across the sky from east to west, which direction do the stars go?" Levi has never forgotten that riddle. It was so dumb he literally waited for a cloudless night to convince himself they went the same way.

After that, he started looking for the familiar constellations every clear night that he was out here. He liked the easy ones like the really big Big Dipper and the little Little Dipper. And Orion was pretty easy to spot with his three-star belt and his very favorite named star, Betelgeuse, at the top left of Orion. He could find the "M or W", and the "House" and his other favorite constellation, the "Ice Cream Cone." It was easy to find because the bright star, Arcturus, was at the tip of the cone.

He would sit out here at night with Blackie sometimes and just fish while he listened to the splash of shrimp or mullet or some other small school of fish trying to escape before something bigger could catch them. He would listen to fiddler crabs crawl around over the mud where the tide had carried the water away leaving the pungent odor of marshland, covered with these miniature lopsided crabs and periwinkle snails. Despite their size and odd claws, there was no doubt that a fiddler crab still looks exactly like a crab but with an oversized claw that looks from a distance like a little fiddle. That, Levi figured, he would never understand. Periwinkle snails clung to sawgrass stalks. He wondered why they did that. He never actually saw one move, but they did. Slower than a regular snail, he suspected.

He liked it here. His dad had taken him to the Okefenokee Swamp Park once so he could learn about the kinds of dangerous animals that were around from the park ranger. Dad said once he thought God must have had it in for this place at some point because there was about every kind of annoying pest to poisonous snakes and humongous spiders, and if that wasn't enough, he had seen alligators big enough to drag you into the river. The no-see-ums were the worst of all. They looked like a small splinter-sized speck, but they would land on you and then crawl around, which you could feel and was annoying, until they found a place to bite you, then they'd just stay there biting you until you had to kill them. He heard his dad tell the mayor once, "If you're not going to try to kill some of these no-see-ums, would you at least feed them every once in a while?" To make matters worse, it never got cold enough to kill them off in winter, so they were hungry every day all year round. Dad said, "Just like me."

It was time to go in after he got the old Coke bottle out of the creek. As he pulled the net in, he saw the bottle inside. He laid the net out on the dock and was fishing out the bottle as Blackie pounced on one shrimp and while holding it down, reached over with his other paw to stop another one from getting away. His legs were so far apart he looked ridiculous. He managed to stop them from getting away before he could get to them, though. Levi saw the old bottle had a tight lid on it and there was something inside of it that looked like a piece of paper. Levi tipped it up and saw there was water in it, too. He guessed it probably was just trash anyway but he still wanted to open it and see.

He stretched the net out on the dock to dry, picked up the ice chest holding the shrimp and carried it and the bottle up to the house. His dad met him outside. "How'd you do?" he asked.

"Good," Levi said. "There's some crabs out there, too," he added.

"Okay, I'll go get 'em. I've got the water boiling," Dan said as he headed out to the dock.

CHAPTER TWO

Abby Mortenson and her mom, Helen, were waiting at the Biscayne Bay Marina in Miami Beach with her dad, Tony, for her dad's best friend, Maurice, to arrive to begin their long boat trip to Baltimore, Maryland. The seagulls were actively flying around and a few pelicans were sitting on pylons waiting patiently for that occasional easy meal from the local fishermen. Abby looked up and watched as a few seagulls started fighting, squawking and flying into each other's way over some dead fish already thrown into the water by a returning boat a few boat slips up from them. The pungent odors of old lingering fish smells brought flocks of seagulls swooping nearby regularly, leaving and returning, looking for something else to eat. The day was warm and the water gently slapped the sides of the boats along the busy marina as the morning temperature was still comfortable in the mid-70s.

Abby was busy at the edge of the dock, when her mom looked up to check on her. She was leaning over the railing, looking for fish. At 10 years old, she not only had a lot of energy but she was also inquisitive. She gave a quick look around to see if anyone was watching before she spit foamy saliva onto the water's surface a few feet below and watched the small minnows come up to see if it's food, like fish tank fish do to fish food. She thought it was weird that they do the same thing here before even knowing what they might be eating. "Yuck," she said out loud as she watched them coming in slowly to try it then propelling themselves away with a swoosh of their tails. She heard her mom call and that broke her attention from the activity in the water below and she ran to her mother who was storing supplies on board their boat.

Abby's dad, Tony, finished storing some supplies away and looked up from what he was doing and scanned the activity going on already on this beautiful sunny morning. It was a perfect day to be on the water. He took a deep breath. He loved the smell of the sea. He knew that odor and could separate it from the more overpowering lingering fishy stench that was not unpleasant to him either. Coming back here always reminded him of how much he missed the ocean when he hadn't been out in a while. Now he was looking for his sunglasses. The glare off the surface of the water was already blinding. His eyes were squinted tight but they were still watering up.

"Here they are," Helen said, "on top of the fridge."

Tony and Maurice were best friends. They played football together at Florida State and they both had been drafted into the NFL and both had made the cut for their teams. Maurice was a Miami Dolphin, while Tony was a brand new Baltimore Raven. He had been to this great seafood restaurant in the mall right on the waterfront at Inner Harbor in Baltimore when he was up there negotiating a great five year contract. Both of them were multimillionaires now. Life was good. He wanted to pull his beautiful boat right up to that dock beside the Seven Foot Knoll Lighthouse and have dinner at McCormick & Schmick's Seafood, and when they were finished, just putter off to the dock at his new home which he hadn't found yet, but he couldn't wait. He decided Helen could have any house she wanted as long as he could get to it with this boat he had grown to love. Besides, he thought it was easier getting around to some places in Baltimore this way than sitting in traffic all the time.

Tony was helping stow food, bed linens and pillows on the refurbished and upgraded 1981 34' Chb Trawler Double Cabin Cruiser when Maurice arrived with his arms full of things to stow. He brought his fishing gear and an extra foldout chair with the fabric bearing the logo of the Miami Dolphins.

There was plenty of room for four and all the supplies they would need. It also had twin 120 HP Lehman diesel engines. The cabin would sleep seven and was beautifully built. The exterior was fiberglass trimmed with beautiful Burmese teak. Inside the cabin, the beautiful teak wood continued throughout and glistened. He had bought it to take on a fishing trip off the NC coast that was coming up soon. He needed to move it from Miami to Baltimore anyway. He fell in love with it and decided, if he could get his friend to come along, he'd like to take it up the coast with his family. He'd been out on it a few times and it was so spacious and comfortable that he talked the family into coming along. The plan was to leave Helen and Abby with her friends at Myrtle Beach and he and Maurice would be going on to enter the 58th Big Rock Blue Marlin tournament, out of Morehead City, NC, with a top prize of 1.6 million dollars. Tony had talked Maurice into going because he knew more about boat motors. He told Maurice that he was sure he wouldn't want his best friend to be stranded at sea because of something breaking on the motor that a piece of duct tape could repair, "Now do ya?" he added, and that he was of the opinion that, "It's fishing for a REALLY big fish for a REALLY lot of money! It's got to be fun! If you don't enter, you can't win!" and flashed his big grin. Maurice agreed, he wanted to go anyway. After the tournament, they planned to come back, maybe with 1.6 million dollars more than they left with, pick up Helen and Abby, and go on to Baltimore's Inner Harbor.

Tony notified the Coast Guard at the base on the causeway of their schedule and route and everyone was ready to get started out across the smooth waters of the inlet. First they wanted to have a good breakfast at the marina diner. There they talked to a couple of regulars and had some selfies taken with a few fans. A few more fans and friends arrived and followed them to the docks, talking about how much they were going to miss them and to come back. The four of them boarded the great boat that Tony was so proud of and pulled away as their friends yelled, "Bon voyage!" and waved bye from the dock. Tony beeped the horn on the beautiful boat, startling a couple of pelicans to leave their perch as they cruised out slowly away from the marina and their friends waving goodbye.

The rest of the day was beautiful. The waters were a little choppy but the cabin cruiser rode like a Harley Electra Glide on a country highway. Helen was making sandwiches while Abby, properly coated in suntan lotion, lay on the deck trying to soak up a couple of rays that might actually get through all the lotion. Tony and Maurice opened their first beer of the trip as they surveyed the ocean around them with no land in sight. As the sun dipped below the horizon, Tony switched on the lights. The running lights only lit a small area and the sky was cloudy enough to limit visibility much further. Abby felt a chill so she sat down close to her dad.

It was nighttime and the heat of the day had zapped everyone's energy. They were cruising along about 25-30 miles offshore. The moon was only visible occasionally between the clouds. The Furuno radar began to beep. Tony was confused when he saw the screen.

"Maurice, come look at this," he said. The swells began to grow. Suddenly, out of the darkness, came the bright light of the moon that had just become visible from behind a heavy cloud set and cast light on a tremendous wall of water coming right at them. A wave no less than 30 feet high began to lift the vessel up like a fast approaching tornado. The cruiser engines whined high as the propellers came momentarily out of the water and then slammed back down into the curling wave. The boat surged up as the props caught the wave. Screams pierced the raging waters.

"Hold on to something!" Tony yelled. For a moment the boat disappeared beneath the cool waters. It rolled completely over beneath the surface of the rough seas. The entire boat had submerged, struggled for buoyancy and up-righted itself nearly full of water as the wave passed. The water behind the wave was calmer but remained rough and covered in foam. The cabin door was closed during the ordeal. The closed door kept it from immediately filling with water and helped upright the boat to bring them back to the surface.

The straining diesels had screamed and choked in the raging water until the boat submerged and then the two massive diesel engines sputtered to a dead silence. The 17,000-pound cruiser sat low, barely afloat. Tony was close enough to grab Abby only a moment before the giant wave hit the defenseless boat. Helen's scream could be heard above the turbulent crashing of rushing water.

"Helen!" Tony yelled.

"Help!" she cried out.

Maurice had managed to grab a rope and ride out the unremorseful ocean's version of a death spin. Now with as much water as was in it, he was able to swim to where Helen was barely clinging to the anchor rope with her arm wrapped around it and her hand tightly grasping the thin line. He reached her outstretched hand just as a wave pounded her face and head, causing her to gasp a nose full of salty water. His hand closed around hers just as she lost her grip on the rope. Tony held onto Abby and moved quickly over to help Maurice. Helen had hit her head and wasn't able to help much. The three of them worked together to get her back inside the floating boat, except now, it was 80 percent under water as waves continued to rock and spill over into the mostly submerged boat. The life raft was still tied down. Tony, with Abby in tow, made it to the life raft and began to untie the lines and wrapped the lifeboat rope around his arm to hold it as steady as he could. "We need to get as much food and drink as we can find," Tony said, assessing the bleak situation they were in. Tony pulled the lifeboat close and wrapped the rope several more times around his arm as Maurice began throwing food into it. When it looked like they may be able to stay afloat, Tony kept the lifeboat ready in case something else happened. Tony told Abby to stay close as he tried to find the bilge pump and get it started. Water continued to come over the low sides now with every wave that came by. The boat's buoyancy was all that had saved them. Abby and Maurice worked furiously to dip water out with a couple of buckets. The waters began to calm.

"What was that," Maurice yelled, "a tsunami wave?"

"I don't know!" Tony yelled back, "It could have been a 'rogue wave.' I've seen videos of where they have been seen over 100 feet high!" Abby was crying so Helen swam over to where she was. It only took Tony one look around to know they were in big trouble. Tony and Maurice were drenched and looked like their life had been drained from them. They knew they had to hold together to survive and they knew each other well enough to know they would both do whatever they could to help each other survive this disaster. Both men put on a brave face but knew their calamity couldn't be more serious.

It wasn't long before the uncontrolled rocking caused Helen and Maurice to begin violently retching over the side. Tony felt so bad for them both. Their seasickness just made everything worse. He went to get the Dramamine patches he saw in the cabin. They were still dry and he hoped they worked to help Helen and Maurice stop the incessant vomiting.

After helping them to open the package and applying one behind an ear, he went into the motor section and struggled to get the bilge pump out from the engine compartment and out of the water. He hoped it would still work as he was hooking it up. The battery was secure enough, everything stayed connected. He lifted the bilge pump and battery out above the waterline, turned it on and began pumping water out. The others were dipping water out as fast as they could in hopes they could get enough out that the waves would stop breaching the sides. They worked together and the ocean's waters remained calm the rest of the night. By daybreak, the boat was emptied of 2/3 of the water and riding higher. Chances looked good that they may not drown or get eaten by sharks, which made Tony feel a little better. He had stopped using the battery for the pump to save energy and helped continue to dip water out. The cabin was a total mess, having been turned upside down and flooded. Some stuff floated while everything else cluttered the floor in the remaining foot of water, rolling from side to side with the movement of the boat inside the cabin. Everyone helped sort through what was salvageable and edible. They were dead in the water though, and at the mercy of the weather and the currents. Now it was about survival.

Tony felt the responsibility for this although no one could have imagined something like this happening. Helen could see the look on his face when he saw her,

"What have I gotten us into?" he asked her woefully.

She put her arm around him and told him she loved him, and told him he damn well better figure out how to get them home. "Oh, by the way, we're selling the boat," she added. She kissed him and began picking things out of the water. He saw the gaunt look on her face from the feeling of constant nausea she was having. She went back to the side of the boat and he could hear her straining to empty her already empty stomach.

They still had most everything they came with. All the supplies in containers remained okay. He found the four five-gallon containers of water that had been secured to the boat and containers of fruit, veggies, sandwich meats and condiments. The bread was ruined and the cookies except for a package of Keebler Oatmeal Sandies that were still sealed. The small refrigerator was a mess, smelling of dill pickles. He picked up the broken glass and threw it all overboard. When he came out of the cabin to toss away the glass, he brought out the cookies and held them up for Abby to see and smiled at her.

She said, "Yuck." He smiled more because these were his favorites not hers, hers were gone.

"Too bad, but I'll share them," he said. He was glad that Abby wasn't getting seasick.

By afternoon, the water was nearly all out of the tight boat and they had mostly dried everything left on board. They ate a small dinner to begin rationing. The sea-sickness patches had finally helped stop the nausea and keeping busy also helped. Maurice had spent the entire day dipping water from the pool down around the motor. He cut off the gas lines and capped the tanks to prevent any water from contaminating the gas before he disconnected anything. He had a smidgen of hope that they may be able to dry the insides of at least one of these engines enough to get it to fire. He knew that these diesel engines were tough and that was enough to keep him working on drying as much of everything he could reach.

The rest of them stayed out of the direct sunlight to prevent dehydration while starting to conserve water. All of the electronics on the older boat were ruined and all the cell phones were lost. There was nothing to do but listen for another boat or plane. Abby and Helen were never out of arm's reach. Maurice was struggling on the motor, taking one piece off at a time, cleaning and drying each piece. Any electronic ignition may be ruined but he didn't know for sure so he kept trying. Tony was trying to catch a few fish to supplement the quickly diminishing food supply. The rods were still in their racks after the boat flipped so Tony decided to try. He suddenly realized all the fish bait was gone. It was lost during the circus trick, underwater flip with a boat full of passengers without losing anybody, which he bet he couldn't do again. He had to make do.

He caught a small whitey with a chunk of balled up bread that was already ruined. He made a miniature sack to hold the bread and made a few small cuts in the bag to allow some of the bread to disperse in the water, slid a hook through it and it worked great. A whitey, about half a pound, took the bait and was hooked.

Now he had pieces of fish to use as bait. He cut the pieces small, because he didn't want to attract big fish or sharks. He didn't know if that would happen but it sounded reasonable to him. He knew sharks could smell blood in water from great distances which caused him to have nightmares of sharks circling the boat and that scared him. The fishing got a little tougher with smaller fish stealing his bait. He decided to use the same strategy he employed earlier. It worked again. With a barbed hook sticking through the bag containing a small piece of the whitey, Tony was able to pull in three more whiteys and a red snapper. It reminded him of the Jerry Seinfeld joke, "Why are fish thin? …because they eat fish."

They found a dry lighter in a survival kit on board and were able to get the propane tank to work. A loud cheer went up when the burner came on the stove. They ate their fill of fish and shared a can of fruit and a can of veggies and drank water for now. They hadn't eaten much since the capsizing last night. He was thinking about the dinner they just ate. It was funny but it actually turned out to be a good day considering there was nothing else to do but drift. Tony was grateful that everyone was trying to keep each other's spirits up and staying out of the direct sunlight. Tony made it clear to everyone that he would never stop trying to get them all back home.

"Ditto," exclaimed Maurice, coming up out of the engine compartment.

Abby cried herself to sleep after dark. Later in the night, she walked up on the bridge where Tony sat gazing out across the vast darkness, looking for that one lifesaving light from another boat that just may happen by. Tony didn't want to miss any opportunity for rescue. They were drifting without lights for now to conserve energy.

"Hey, honey. You okay?" Tony asked the troubled young girl.

"I want to go home, Daddy, and I want to walk on land and see my friends," she began to weep in her dad's arms.

"I know, sweetheart. I promise to never stop trying to get us home," he said sincerely and kissed her head. "That's why I'm out here," he said in an uplifting tone, "Any minute a big ship may happen by so I'm here to keep a lookout. You just never know when it could happen."

She sat there with him looking at the stars. "There's the Big Dipper," she said pointing toward the constellation.

"And there's Orion," he said. He explained to her how early sailors had instruments called sextants to help them point the right direction to where they were going using the North Star as a guide. We use compasses and GPS now. He told her how sailors would become familiar with the stars and use them like sign posts to remain on course. Knowing that made her feel less lost for some reason; like they were broken down on the side of the road and someone would be driving by sooner or later and would stop to help them. She wanted to keep watch, too.

CHAPTER THREE

Day after hot day passed draining everyone's energy while choppy seas made it difficult to walk, to sit and to sleep at night. They had been floating on this endlessly rocking ocean for over a month and everyone was exhausted. The canned vegetables and most other foods had run out but Tony could still catch fish so they took to drying some out to store for eating later. As the long hot day dragged on, the drying fish odors attracted a lone sea bird. Maurice observed the aggressive bird trying repeatedly to sneak the easy meal of fish lying exposed on the deck drying out in the sun so he made a snare trap and actually caught the little thief in a fish net. Everyone thought that was it awesome how he caught that noisy bird and that evening it was a nice alternative to fish for dinner. Abby thought it was gross but no one complained after Maurice began calling it a flying chicken. After dinner Maurice returned to the engine compartment to try again to get the motor to start. The sea water had gotten into the electrical system but everything was dry now and he had cleaned what he could reach. He even managed to get one motor to turn over once by bypassing the starter. He continued to work on the gas lines and carburetor. He felt like he might be making progress. He tried again, and heard the motor catch for a second time. That motivated him to check the air filter and give it another good wipe down. It was difficult to keep out sea spray while floating around with waves continuing to splash saltwater all over everything.

It was starting to cloud up again. It had rained off and on over the days enough so that they were able to replace some of the water they had drank already with fresh rainwater. The clouds creeping toward them now were dark and heavy with moisture. This one was going to be rough, Tony thought. He looked at Maurice, "Now would be a good time to try to get some control of this boat."

"Okay, let me get everything put back together and I'll be ready to try again," Maurice said as he ducked back down out of sight. The rain was coming. They moved everything back into the cabin. Abby and Helen were already in the cabin stowing dishes and securing cabinets and drawers. The rocking boat was causing them to bump into each other. Abby lost her balance and fell over onto one of the beds. She decided to stay there and ride it out. After the last dish was put away, Helen grabbed a life jacket for the both of them. Without a word, they both put them on. The wind was picking up and white caps topped the waves as the winds rocked the boat. Gray clouds filled the sky above them as the boat began to be tossed around.

Maurice came up out of the engine area. "Keep your fingers crossed!" he yelled over the increasing winds. He touched his screwdriver to the starter directly, a spark flashed and the motor turned over...once...then it caught and came to life.

"Oh my God!" Tony yelled. Maurice's face lit up like Publisher's Clearing House was at his door. "Let's get out of here."

Helen came out and was ecstatic to hear the motor start. Tony manned the helm and looked at the compass. It still had water in it and he couldn't tell if it was working. Right now he was just trying to turn into the waves as the wind and rain started to pelt the boat. He steered the large boat with one working engine to ride the waves to keep it from listing past the point of no return again. Brief respites from the rain and strong winds gave Tony the time he needed to regroup and reposition his vessel into the wind. The boat held together and survived the onslaught of wind and waves even though the motor was not sounding so good. It was sputtering as if it couldn't get good compression or maybe the gas had saltwater in it. It would just bog down when he tried to give it gas. The saltwater had damaged some of the filters and gaskets and all of the electronics. Maurice wasn't sure how long it was going to keep going. It needed some new parts but for now they had to make do with what they had.

Finally, the winds died down and Tony headed as west as he thought he could get by looking at the damaged compass. He thumped the compass with his finger and could tell that the needle wasn't moving freely inside. He could see moisture on the glass inside and corrosion forming around the edge. He knew that both of those things were probably interfering with its normally smooth motion. He was having trouble with that and the sky was overcast. As nightfall came, he began to have doubts that he was going in the right direction. He wasn't sure anymore.

Maurice had helped Helen catch a couple more fish for dinner but she couldn't stomach another bite of fish even though now that was all they had. She had passed a few other times already. The nausea from earlier bouts of seasickness had already caused her to lose fluids and weight.

The next day Tony spotted an island. He had no idea where they were but the consensus was that being on land was better than being lost in the ocean. Drifting out at sea for so long had caused all of them to lose weight. Maurice and Tony were athletes who normally worked out vigorously every day but now after many days of reduced caloric intake and inactivity, their massive muscles had shrunk to that of regular guys. When he looked at Abby, she was very thin now. He started looking for a sandy place to get up next to the shore. He was also thinking that maybe he and Maurice could more easily work on the boat if it wasn't rocking all the time.

It was a medium-sized island with trees and no signs of life from here. There were no buildings or boats around. It appeared to be maybe a mile or so wide and thick with foliage. It looked like there was a good chance of finding water and maybe some fruit. That would be good, he thought. There was also a high point on the island. He would figure out some sort of fire signal in case a ship or plane flew close enough to spot them. He told everyone to get ready to kiss the sand. "I will!" Abby yelled, and squealed an eleven-year-old girl's playground scream. Tony felt his eardrums vibrate.

They weren't sure if it was completely uninhabited. They could at least get off the boat and look around. They all wanted to do that. He made his way toward the island. The struggling diesel engine, no matter how durable, was damaged and could stop at any moment. Maybe on shore they could work on it together.

He found a sandy shore and coasted up to it. "I hate to turn it off," Tony said.

"I know but we can't just leave it running," said Maurice, "Do you think it will restart?"

Tony hesitated and said, "I don't know."

"Now is as good a time as any time. We aren't going anywhere," Maurice finished.

"Don't say that," Tony said as he killed the motor. The sounds instantly changed. They could hear birds calling from the deep jungle. The ocean waves casually rolled in. Helen and Abby were out of the boat before it stopped, trying to get rid of their sea legs. They both started laughing at each other when they tried to walk on land. It felt so strange and Abby felt off balance. How long had it been, Tony wondered, weeks at least. He knew that things weren't great, just much improved. Abby was running down the beach now. "Don't go out of sight," he heard Helen call to her.

Tony and Helen started exploring along the beach area. Tony was checking everything out. He was observing the ocean near the shore for possible fishing areas and the shoreline for fruit trees and maybe a freshwater branch or spring. They were counting the coconuts they saw, so far about a dozen plus a few mango trees. Tony guessed the island to be mostly round and about two miles in diameter with the high point was in the middle. Rain water had to go somewhere so he decided to keep walking. Before they went too far, Helen decided to go back and stay with Abby. Tony knew there had to be a stream somewhere coming off that hill. That's what he wanted to find so he started walking.

Maurice went into the forest a short distance to become familiar with the area. He was looking for anything they could use. He knew they would need wood for fire and water. He kept his eyes and ears open for any signs or sounds of running water. The dense growth on the ground and vines running up trees hid much that was underneath. He knew there was a high point on the island so he headed that way. He saw a few lizards and insects along the way that were intimidatingly large.

He moved through the natural openings in the jungle, dragging and stomping down foliage to make it easier to find his way back. He imagined King Kong or a large prehistoric saber-tooth tiger about to leap out on him. "Get a grip," he said to himself. There were many vines and he saw things hanging from some trees that he thought might be some kind of fruit but he couldn't name it. He came to the foot of the hill where it was somewhat rocky. He started around the base and hadn't gone far before finding a small stream. He reached down for a handful of the cool water and tried it. It tasted fresh and delicious. It was the first water he'd had that hadn't tasted like the plastic container it came out of in weeks. He got a couple of good handfuls and started to follow the stream toward the shore. About 50 yards ahead he found a water basin full of fresh water about 20 feet across and crystal clear. The stream continued on. As he came out onto the beach, he heard a loud voice. "Hey! Hey! Over here!" Tony yelled when he saw him walking out of the jungle.

"Hey," called Maurice back. Tony had made it all the way to where Maurice had followed the stream out of the jungle.

"Find anything?" Tony asked.

"Yep, there's plenty of fresh water and probably enough fruit to keep us going awhile," Maurice said, trying to sound upbeat.

"Good. Let's go back to the others and decide what we want to do," Tony said.

Abby was playing along the beach and exploring the edge of the forest while Helen watched her and silently prayed that they were rescued. She hated the thought of anything happening to Abby. She had such high hopes and dreams. Abby wanted to be a dancer and dance on stage. She had a routine where she would pirouette and then plié, then a group of three jumps with half turns, landing softly and ending the routine with a graceful arabesque. Helen knew she would be a beautiful dancer one day.

When Tony and Maurice came back into view of the others down the beach, Abby ran to meet them. "Did you find anything?" she asked excitedly.

"Yep, we did. We found a McDonald's!" he said but his smile told Abby he was kidding.

"No, you didn't!" she said.

He laughed and said, "Well, we did find some fresh water and some fresh fruit."

"Oh goody!" she screamed and ran back toward her mom, yelling, "They found water and fruit, Mommy!"

"Great!" Tony heard Helen call back. They came back to where Helen was laying out some leftover fish for the men. They ate standing up and discussed where they should set up a camp.

Tony started by saying, "I'm guessing it would be convenient to be closer to the stream of freshwater." Maurice added that they needed to always be looking out in the ocean for that speck that might be a boat. He was afraid they could easily miss a boat that may come by. They'd have to keep watching day and night anyway. They both decided that any rescue fire should be high on the hill and easy to spot on any side of the island. Tony and Maurice pushed the heavy boat out away from the shore and pulled it along the shoreline in the direction of the freshwater stream. Once there, they began to unload a few things they could use.

Maurice walked into the edge of the forest and began to drag a few dead limbs and palm fronds out to the beach and pile them up. Tony opened the diesel can and dipped a stick into it. He lit the stick and placed it in a good spot to light the fronds and twigs on fire. Once it was lit they placed a few more limbs on the fire and had dinner that this time included some fresh coconut and mangoes. After dinner, they all boarded the boat and Tony pushed it out away from the shore about 50 feet and dropped anchor. He felt like they were safer out here on the boat and it put some distance between them and the flying and crawling things on shore until they could explore the rest of the island and come up with a better plan.

That night was quiet. Small waves slapped the boat rhythmically. One startled Abby awake. She got up without disturbing her parents and sat on the deck looking toward the island. It was very dark and scary at night and noises from the animals became louder. All the frogs and insects were forcefully spewing out their sounds. To Abby it sounded like there were thousands of them and that each one was trying to be the loudest. Suddenly a fish jumped out of the water and hit the side of the boat causing Abby to jump. She turned away from the island to look out at sea. She didn't see a single light on the horizon as far as she could see in any direction.

The stars were so bright and there were so many, she became lost in looking at them all. She saw the Big Dipper and then she saw a shooting star flash by. "Ha!" she gasped and remembered to make a wish. Suddenly she remembered something. She had seen a plastic Coke bottle in the boat. She remembered thinking if she put a note inside of it and threw it out in the ocean maybe someone would find it and rescue them. She started to think about what she should put on the note. She found an old piece of paper that had dried well enough to write on but the pen was splotchy. She wanted to try anyway.

She wrote:

Help!!! Alive!!!

Tony, Helen, Abby Mortenson

Marice Munz

Left Miami June 5 2016 for Mrtle Beach

On an iland. We are lost. At night I see these stars.

Giant wave.

Then she drew a rough outline of a map the shape of Florida and a circle out in the ocean where she thought they might be. She tried to match the map Dad drew in the sand when he and Maurice were trying to figure out where they were. She had drawn the Big Dipper and Orion's Belt on the map as well because Dad said ships used to use them to sail by. She didn't want to leave anything out. She felt a little embarrassed in doing this but she wanted to try so she didn't tell anyone. She stood on the stern at the edge of the rail and was watching the waves as she heard someone coming up on deck. She hid the bottle behind a chair.

"Are you okay?" Helen asked.

"Yeah," Abby said, "I just saw a shooting star."

"Yeah? I hope you wished us a way home," Helen said as she looked up, "The sky is really incredible."

CHAPTER FOUR

Levi had taken the note out of the bottle and set the bottle on a shelf, but the note was still a mystery. It was wet and the writing was mostly blurred out. He heard his dad coming back in the house and coming to his door carrying a bucket with blue crabs in it, clicking their claws. "These are going to be good," Dan said. "Hey Dad, look what I found inside this bottle," as he held up the small piece of damp paper. His dad looked from the doorway. "What's that?" Dan asked. "It's a note or something. I don't know but it's strange," Levi answered. Dan agreed it was interesting. "Keep working on it. Flatten it out and let it dry," Dan said.

So far Levi could make out one thing... Alive! Then the next row, Helen and Abby, then the next line was something, M---z. Then the next line, something about Myrtle Beach, then the next line was something...island, something else. Some spelling errors but he was pretty sure that was what it said. Then numbers on the next line, June 5 2015, then a picture of what looked like the outline of Florida and then dots were on the side. At the bottom were words he felt were pretty easy to read and their meaning was clear, too. It said, "Giant Wave." He felt the hair stand up on his arms and neck.

"Are you ready to eat some crabs?" his dad asked from his door. "Sure!" Levi said as he brought the note with him to the table. Levi took the note and flattened it out beside his plate with his hand so it would dry quicker. He was ready to crack some crabs and peel some shrimp but he kept looking at the note trying to figure out what it meant.

Steam encircled the kitchen and the blue crabs were bright red now. Old Bay seasoning coated them as Dad took them one at a time out of the big crab pot he used to boil them in. He had added Louisiana Crab Boil for added seasoning. After cooling for a few minutes they sat there using pliers and a small hammer to crack the legs open. He could tell the males from the females by looking at the bottom. The males had a kind of tab looking portion that he would use almost like a tab on a can to separate the shell from the body to get to the white tender meat inside. Picking the delicious white meat out of the crab's legs was a slow, tedious job but when eating crab, they were in no hurry.

His dad asked about the note lying beside Levi's plate, "Did you figure out what that is?"

"Dad, look at this! It's a note. It was inside that bottle I caught in my net."

"Okay," Dan said. He started to reach for it and then looked at his fingers, "Let's finish eating first."

"Okay," Levi agreed as he looked at his own fingers. He picked up another big claw and cracked it with his pliers. He was able to separate the two halves, leaving the entire edible portion intact. He dipped it into some melted butter and added a little more Old Bay for good measure. His mouth started watering the moment it hit his tongue. Neither spoke for a while as the two of them sat at the counter cracking crabs together, concentrating on getting as much as possible of the tiniest bits of crab meat out of the convoluted shells.

After dinner and a quick clean-up of the kitchen, they sat back down at the table. Levi took the now mostly dry piece of paper and laid it on the table under the bright overhead light so the both of them could look at it together.

Levi started, "Looks like, "Help!" then, "Alive!" He'd figured the top line out. There was a row before the row that said Helen then Abby. He couldn't make it out. Started with T something space and a longer word, maybe an M, he guessed. Then below Helen and Abby was...something...island and something else.

"These numbers look like a date, June 5 2015 or 16," his dad added. Then Levi saw the rough map of Florida with the circle and the constellations.

"What does that have to do with anything?" Levi asked. He could see the bottom part much better now that it was dry. He pulled out his magnifying glass and looked closely at the part below the map. "Here," Levi said, "What do you think this says?"

Dan took the small piece of paper and held it up to the light and said, "Looks like it says: Left Miami for Myrtle Beach, SC." He scrutinized it more closely and was able to read more. He said, "I can't read some of it but I can read the words, Giant Wave. And the names at the top looked like Tony, Helen and Abby M..., something, then, a smeared line. Mauric, and something about an island." Now Dan was curious as well.

"Dad?" Levi asked, "Do you think this is legit? Do you think someone is calling for help?"

"I don't know, Levi," Dan said.

CHAPTER FIVE

Tony and Maurice made a decision that they would try to get and keep the boat able to start but not leave unless they spotted a low flying airplane or another boat that they may be able to flag down easier if they could get out on the water. On shore they had HELP spelled out in huge letters made of logs and rocks and they had been leaving the boat away from shore to make it easier to spot by air as well. There were also three flares in the emergency kit but they had gotten wet and they weren't sure if they would even work, but they had them and would try to use them at night if a plane or ship came by. Unfortunately, they hadn't seen nor heard anything coming their way since they got here. On the highest point of the hill, an area was cleared and made ready for a bonfire. A tall stack of small dried branches and grasses that should catch fire quickly were bunched together and ready to be lit from early evening until the sun rose. A container of diesel fuel sat nearby to get it going fast. Beside that was a 20-foot-tall tree post they stuck in the ground with a half bed sheet at the top of it like a flag to be seen easier during the day. They came up together every morning to check that the flag wasn't tangled and the materials to start the fire quickly were always ready.

As Abby walked through the wooded area to the pool, she saw movement ahead. She thought it was her mom. Not stopping, she walked right out into the clearing. Then the two of them saw each other at the same time and both froze, staring. Abby couldn't believe what her eyes were seeing. Her mouth dropped open and she couldn't move or say anything.

"Hello!" came from the frozen person with extremely pale skin, who was standing in the shallow edge of the water. She thought she was looking at a ghost.

"Aaaaaahhhh!" she gasped, startled to see anyone, especially someone who was as white as a sheet.

"Who are you?" Abby called out. The startled being still had not moved since he saw her. She was not 20 feet away.

"I'm Michael," the unusual-looking boy swallowed and answered back in a calm voice without moving a muscle. They stood there looking at each other, not knowing what to say next. Abby stared at him. He was completely as white as a sheet of paper wearing a swimsuit.

"You can speak English?" she asked.

"Yes. Why? What do you mean? I learned it in school. What's wrong with English?" asked Michael. "You're speaking English. What's wrong with English?" he asked. She just stood there.

"No, English is fine. Good. Where did you come from?" Abby asked.

"Here, I live here," Michael got in quickly.

"You don't live here. No one lives here," she said.

"Yes, I do. Well, out there," he pointed out toward the beach.

"What do you mean?" she wasn't quite getting it.

"Yes, underwater," he said. "In Atlantis," Michael tried to explain.

"Atlantis, that lost city in the movie? There's no such place," she said, stunned.

"No, not THE lost city, that's the name my grandparents named OUR city. I was born there. What's your name?" Michael asked.

"Abby," she answered. "I never saw anyone so white before."

"I know," he answered. "I'm not supposed to be here right now because you weren't supposed to see me. But, since you are here and aren't going anywhere, well...can I trust you?" He surprised her by asking that.

"Yes," she said.

"Okay, I know people here don't believe in aliens. Well, some do. Anyway, I'm not an alien but my parents are," he began. Abby couldn't stop staring at him. Her mouth hung open a little as she listened to his story.

"My family came here from another planet outside this solar system in 1947," he started. "I've seen you already and I know you are castaways," he went on. "Would you like to know about how we got here?"

Abby sat down to listen. "Yeah!" she said.

"Have you ever heard of Roswell, New Mexico?" He began telling an incredible tale, repeating stories he had heard describing how his family came here in the 40s looking for a new home after traveling centuries through space until they found and then made it to Earth. "We couldn't live up here on land because our grandparents were afraid to be seen by those already here, but we come up here sometimes," Michael said. "We've been here on this island a long time."

"Why haven't we seen you sooner?" Abby asked.

"Because we knew you were here. Once we realized you weren't leaving, we weren't allowed to come up here," Michael explained.

"You came up here," Abby said, pointing out the obvious fact that he was here after being told not to come.

"Yes, I like to come up here. I've seen you before, but I hid so you couldn't see me. This time you sneaked up on me," he said smiling.

Abby smiled as well, and then a serious look came over her face. "Do you know where we are?" she asked. "I mean, can you help us get home? We can't get home," she slowly asked and looked at him intently.

"I don't know what I can do," he said.

"I put a note in a bottle last night but I haven't thrown it out in the water yet. I was going to last night but I got interrupted. I know it doesn't have a chance," she finished.

"You put a message in a bottle? Do you know where it is?" Michael asked.

"Yes, why?" she asked.

"Maybe I can take it to where you want it to go without being seen," Michael suggested.

"Do you mean deliver it?" she asked.

"Yes, but I can't guarantee anything because I can't be seen," Michael explained.

Then Abby had another thought. "Can I see Atlantis?" she asked.

"Oh no, I don't think I can get you in without someone seeing you," Micheal answered.

"I bet YOU could," she said.

"Let me think about it," he said.

"Do you know how far we are from Florida?" Abby asked.

"How far, I don't know," he said. "But it wouldn't take long to get there and back and deliver the package. That sounds like a spy job. This will be fun!"

"You're funny," Abby said.

"No, it's just that I like spy movies," Michael explained. "I want to go to New York and see if anyone notices me. I always heard we could walk around there without anyone even caring about us," he said. "I sneak in close sometimes. Once, I got really close to the shore in Savannah. I'm good," he boasted to Abby. "You should have seen how close. I could have been 007. The Daniel Craig one, not the Pierce Brosnan one," Michael pointed out.

Abby looked at him in amazement. "You like James Bond?" she asked.

"Duh!" he answered.

"Okay, Bond, James Bond, how close?" Abby asked.

"Okay, okay, I was headed toward Savannah but I can only see the shoreline and things in the water on my scanner. I didn't really want to go into Savannah but on St. Patrick's Day I drifted really close and saw how crowded and crazy that place gets. I just drifted out in front of everybody and no one noticed a thing. It was noisy with loud music and people talking and yelling and horns and sirens. It was great."

"Sounds crazy," Abby said.

Suddenly something else occurred to Abby, "Hey! You said you were born here in Atlantis? I'm pretty sure we're still in America. Then, you're not only an Earthling, you may be an American!"

"That's funny!" Michael said.

Abby smiled. "We could be in the same class at school," she realized. "Can I introduce you to my family?" she asked.

"Oh no, that could be bad for us," Michael said. There was a pause and then he added with a serious look on his face, "My dad said President Obama may make us start paying taxes."

Abby thought that was funny and said, "My dad would say, you probably would get money. Ha ha!" They laughed at their parents. "Besides, it might be ok. This is America, land of the free," Abby said. "Oh yeah?" Michael retorted, "What's free? Everything costs a fortune here." "I'm not talking about free stuff, Michael, I'm talking about "free-dumb, which means you're free to ask "dumb" questions," Abby shot back. Michael looked at her and she looked at him. The corners of their lips started turning up and Michael burst out laughing.

Things got quiet for a few seconds, and then Abby asked, "Where are you from?"

"Atlantis, I told you!" Michael said.

"I mean...where are you from? Like what planet?" she struggled to get it out.

"Earth!" he laughed.

"Okay, okay...I won't ask anymore."

"Dad says our safety is too important. Right now, we stay around here," Michael finished saying. "Anyway, it's ancient history and you wouldn't know it. We call it Tyrol, it was our home planet. We left Tyrol because it became so dry, it was impossible to stay. There was not enough water there. You can imagine how excited our parents and grandparents were to see the big blue Earth out at the edge of this galaxy. They were so happy. When they realized it was inhabited, they couldn't risk being turned away and then the damage on entry. We came in unseen and stayed right where we landed, underwater. The spaceship that crashed in Roswell was one of our scout ships. No one has ever found us." Abby listened to the incredible story being told by Michael like stuff like that happened every day.

"Well, tell me how I can help you and I'll try," Michael said.

"Okay", she said. "I'll see if I can find the map. I know we have some on the boat. Can you meet me back here later?" she asked excitedly.

"I can come back about this time tomorrow," Michael answered.

"You know, you could pass for human, except for your head being bald and so white," Abby observed.

"Thanks," he said. "Maybe I'll get a tan and a wig when I get to Miami!" Michael said as he surprised Abby further by saying that some of his friends and family had done that and were living there now.

"What?" Abby asked.

"Why not, we're Earthlings! You just didn't know we were here. What if flying over some desolate part of Antarctica, you found a village? And when you went in there, you found a completely self-sufficient society in some ways ahead of your own," Michael said.

"I never thought of that, but your grandparents are aliens!" Abby said.

"I know that," Michael stated, "my parents too, that's why we have to slowly move our families into the U.S., only a couple at the time. We give them all the stuff they need. They've been watching satellite TV for years. They know almost anything you could ask them. One even tried out for Jeopardy but didn't get on the show. Too bad, too, this guy is really smart."

Abby didn't know what to make of all this. She listened to Michael. He looked odd but he was every bit American, the way he talked, his mannerisms and everything else she could think of.

After he left, Abby ran back to camp so her mom wouldn't be

worried and send her dad looking for her. She knew he would come over here first so she got back and began looking for things to do to help out.

"Where've you been?" her mom asked.

"At the pool," she answered, "I like it there."

Helen watched her ten-year-old daughter. There were so many things she wanted to do with her and classes to take. She hoped she didn't get too far behind in her studies. She was glad that she looked happier tonight than she had seen her in a long while. She smiled and said, "Okay, your dad and Maurice will be back in a few minutes with dinner." She had hung a pot of water over the fire pit to get ready for whatever the men could catch.

Abby wanted so much to tell everyone about Michael, but she sat in deep thought during dinner without saying much. Dad said they checked the HELP signal and made sure the fire wood was dry. It looked like rain was coming. They had built a cover for it so it would light even if it was raining. Their dinner was especially good that night. They talked about staying alert to ships that may pass by. Abby said she wanted to help keep watch for ships. Her dad told her just to keep it on her mind and if something caught her eye, stop and look at it again to see if she could tell if it was a ship or plane. She said she would.

CHAPTER SIX

After dinner, Levi was studying the small piece of paper again. He was wondering what it meant. He asked his dad to look at it again, but so far they really didn't know what to do with it. He started wondering about the stars. Why were the stars there? He got up and went outside to sit on the dock with Blackie. It was a clear night. He looked up and the first thing he saw was the Big Dipper and Orion was not far behind. He wondered if the person who wrote this note was looking at the same constellations as he was right now.

Sitting out on the end of the dock, he watched Blackie eating a shrimp he had caught in his net. Shrimp were sparse right now. The current was going out already. He watched small schools of fish slice through the water under the moonlit river. He picked up his net again to try to catch Blackie some of the small mullet swimming in schools. As he threw the net out in the middle of the swift running river, he continued to think about the stars on the note. Then he had a thought. If they were close enough and looking up and he was looking down, he would see them. He was sure it would be an impossible task. He had to try it first. He spread his net out on the deck to dry, leaving Blackie to finish his snack.

He hurried up to his room and sat down at his computer. He pulled out the message and started looking at it again. It looked like a circle with the words HELP and Island. He wondered if the island might be sort of round like that. Then, he had an epiphany. He had what could have possibly been his first "Eureka!" moment.

Perhaps his first original thought derived from scattered information he obtained and was able to logically piece together. He looked at the facts, drew a conclusion and now knew what it meant to "think out of the box", to come up with a logically possible solution. He wondered if it had ever been done or if it was even possible. He wanted to find that island using Google Earth and just search the Atlantic Ocean for this round island with a HELP signal on it.

Levi convinced his dad that this note was from some shipwrecked people and he was going to try to find them using Google Earth. He pulled up the site on his computer and started zooming in. He found the southeast US including all of the Florida, Georgia and South Carolina coastline. He drew an imaginary line in his mind and started moving the cursor out over the ocean and zoomed in as close to Earth as he could zoom in. He knew he could see his own house, he even saw his dad standing near his truck. Dad said that the street level picture was taken from a truck. He saw the Google Earth truck drive by that day. Levi decided he would just scan the ocean and see if he could find them. Since it was nearly all water, it shouldn't take forever. So he began that evening.

His dad knew that if Levi was right it was a long shot to ever find castaways, but his curiosity got the best of him and he began to wonder if it was possible to do that. He sat down at the computer too and tried it. It was incredible, he thought, that you could command a satellite view of the Earth with the capacity to zoom in well enough to see people from your living room. The only thing was that these images were not live shots, they were snapshots taken by the satellite as it passed over an area, so if the images were taken before the note was written there may not be any HELP signal laid out on that beach. He decided he wasn't going to say anything negative about it to Levi. He would just continue to help. He didn't know what exactly he was looking for except an uninhabited small island off the coast, who knew how far north or south. It was a long shot and he knew it was going to take a lot of luck. Then he thought, if there were castaways out there, they were praying for more than a little luck. He knew he would be.

His dad looked at the note again while Levi was scrutinizing the Atlantic Ocean looking for a needle there. He saw what Levi had figured out already. The paper wasn't as damaged as he thought. Once it was dry and flat, it was much easier to read. He saw the date and a route from Miami to Myrtle Beach. He decided he would look in papers online from Miami and see if anything was in them he could gather clues from.

He started with the Miami Herald on June 5th, 2016. Nothing mentioned. The 6th, then the 7th, then on the 10th there it was, on the front page. The story read, "NFL players, Tony Mortenson, Maurice Munoz, Lost At Sea. Tight End for the Baltimore Ravens, his wife Helen, daughter Abby and good friend Maurice Munoz, offensive lineman, who currently is on the active roster for the Miami Dolphins did not arrive at their destination of Myrtle Beach on June 8th. The news report indicated the Cabin Cruiser left during calm conditions while on a route to Myrtle Beach, SC, but never arrived. No distress signal or other contact from the vessel was ever picked up from any source. A search for five days by the US Coast Guard and multiple private vessels combed the high seas searching for the missing vessel. Due to worsening weather, the search was called off five days later; however, an alert was sent out to all vessels in the area to be on AL ERT and to continue to lookout for any stranded vessels or survivors. So far, no signs of wreckage have been found." He looked at the note again. It definitely said Abby and Maurice.

Other online stories hypothesized that the Bermuda Triangle had claimed the boat and its occupants. Stories suggested that it was just another in a long series of disappearances in that part of the ocean that included not only ships but planes. There were stories of planes dating back to WWII when an entire squadron on a training mission had disappeared. There were stories about how electromagnetic fields could cause compasses to spin uncontrollably and planes would run out of gas trying to find land. Most recent stories included rogue waves 100 feet high that could wipe out small boats. There was even a story of one hitting a cruise ship that became the first documented evidence of rogue waves and how their origins had yet to be explained. The story ended like a mystery still unsolved about the lost NFL players and one's family.

CHAPTER SEVEN

The next afternoon, while Maurice and Tony were working on the big boat motors, Abby found her bottle with her note in it she had written the day before and had left behind a chair on the boat. She told her dad she was going for a walk as she headed back to the pool. She sat down and started thinking about Michael and Atlantis. *It must be awesome*, she thought. She wanted to see it. When Michael came back, she ran up to meet him. He had a big smile on his face.

"Hi!" he said, "I've been thinking. Would you like to go for a ride in my supership?"

"You have a supership?" Abby asked.

"Yeah! It can be a sub so fast, nothing can catch it! And it can FLY!" Michael said excitedly.

"Wow!" Abby said, "I could be home in no time if you could take me there."

"I know. I wish I could," Michael agreed.

Abby was amazed when she walked to the edge of the water. The circular object floating just below the surface of the water was about the size of a compact car. It was dark and could only be seen when you were about to step on it, like a stingray lying still on the ocean's floor. "Can I ride in it?"

"Okay, I'll just take you to Savannah and drop you off," Michael said smiling.

"I have my bottle with my note inside," and held it up to show him.

He took the bottle and said, "I'll keep it and take it there tomorrow."

"I wish I could go but I can't leave my family," Abby said.

"If this note thing doesn't work, we'll think of something else," Michael said, "Don't worry." Knowing Michael was going to help them get rescued made Abby feel a lot better. She knew they wouldn't be stranded here forever.

Abby followed Michael into the water. He told her to take a breath and follow him as he dove under the vehicle. She followed closely behind and came up into a hole underneath. Michael pulled himself up and then helped Abby out of the water and handed her an absorbent material to dry off with. She sat in the comfortable seat beside Michael and felt warm air surrounding her in a comfortable environment. There were four seats. He sat in the driver's seat, she rode shotgun. "Seat belt," he said, "it's the law."

"Really?" Abby asked. As she sat, half-reclined in the contoured seat, she saw nothing but darkness in front of her. Then Michael touched an area on the front of the vehicle and she felt it move but heard nothing. She felt the vehicle going forward, then the wall above and before her opened to a panoramic view. The ocean was dark as the motion of the supership stirred up sediment that soon started to settle. Then, as they moved into deeper and clearer water, small and medium sea fish, some colorful tropical fish and jellyfish kept coming into view. There was minimal illumination outside the vehicle. "Where are we going?" Abby asked.

"To see Atlantis, you said you wanted to see it, didn't you?" Michael answered. "I can't take you inside but I can show it to you," Michael said.

"How far is it?" Abby asked.

"It's about 10 miles out," Michael answered.

"Oh no, this could take too long. What if Dad comes looking for me?" she said.

"Okay, we'll make this fast," Michael said. "Hold on!"

Abby held on to her seat and felt a surge forward and then a slowing down like a horizontal elevator. When she looked again she really saw nothing but the sandy, algae-laden ocean floor.

"Can you see it?" Michael asked.

"See what?" Abby asked back.

"Atlantis," Michael answered.

"No, I don't see anything except a few big fish and a shark right over there," she pointed to a hammerhead swimming nearby. Abby sat confused.

"That's right, but it's right here under the sediment and sand with barnacles and sea life on top of it, as far as you can see. It's pretty big inside, like a small city I guess," Michael explained.

Abby couldn't believe it. She could see some areas that looked like there might be something there, but she wasn't sure. "How do you get inside of it?" she asked.

"Right over there," he pointed to what looked like a natural rock outcropping. "I can open it from here," and he pointed to a button on the console.

"Where are the others? Are you the only one out?" she asked.

"Yes, they're around," Michael answered.

She looked around but didn't see any other craft. "Does it fly?" she asked.

"Of course, well, it used to. Every once in a while, they do system checks and it sounds like it runs fine. How do you think we got here? The story goes that when we first came to Earth, our home had undergone so much damage from the heat coming into the atmosphere that we lost power and plummeted into the sea right here. We couldn't leave it so we stayed here. So, it's my home sweet home."

"Wow!" she said.

"Yes, but we have to be careful not to be seen. My dad said he isn't sure if good or bad would come of it," Michael explained.

"Yes, I don't know either except you're in America, which is good. I'm glad," Abby said and smiled at him.

"Me, too," he said. "We better get back." He turned the ship around and headed at supership speed back to the island.

She swam out from under the ship just as her dad was walking down the beach. He saw her coming out of the water. "Hey!" he called, "What cha' doin'?"

She was surprised to see him. "I was just swimming."

"Oh. Okay," he said. "Are you ready for dinner?"

"Yeah!" she called and started running toward him as fast as she could and jumped up into his arms. "You're wet!" he exclaimed as he swung her high in the air. She gave him a big hug when she stopped.

"What was that for?" he asked.

"Cause!" she said.

"Cause you know I love you?" he said.

"I love you!" she said back, "Race you to Mommy!" They both took off running toward the camp.

The next day, Abby spent much of her time by the pool but Michael didn't come.

CHAPTER EIGHT

Dan looked at his son. He watched him scrutinizing the screen of water and more water. A sudden sense of pride caused him to tear up. His son, Levi, was looking for a tiny island in the middle of the ocean for castaways based on finding a message in a bottle. *Unbelievable.* He watched him spend every minute he could staring at the screen and using his mouse to navigate the satellite directions he wanted to view.

Levi's attention was caught up in the images on the screen. He was observing distinct but jagged outlines, clearly visible contrasting blues, aquamarines and various shades of blue and green against the shallower waters. He never realized how many shades of blue there are out there. He saw light blue shallow areas and he could clearly see darker blue waters where the drop offs were. He was contemplating that the blues of the sea made him think of the different hues of the evening sky. He was lost in thought, starting to appreciate why his dad had pointed out these things.

Dan started with a big, "Guess what?" to get Levi's attention. Levi saw he had his laptop in his hands. "Look what I just found," Dan said. He opened the laptop and showed him the news article about the missing football players and the Mortenson family.

Levi couldn't believe it. "It's them!" he said. "They're alive!" Levi shouted.

"Maybe, but that doesn't mean we can find them," his dad tried to bring reality into the picture. "How are you doing with your search? Are you able to see anything?" he asked.

"Yeah," Levi said, "Everything!"

Then Dan asked him, "How would you feel about notifying the Miami Herald? We can send them a copy of the note and see what they think. We might even get to tell their families that there may be hope of finding everyone."

"Yeah!" Levi scanned the note into his computer, saved it on a file and then added it as an attachment on an email addressed to the Miami newspaper:

Please take a look at the attachment to this email. It is a picture of a note that was retrieved from a plastic soda bottle from the saltwater creek behind my house. It may be information regarding the disappearance of NFL players Maurice Munoz and Tony Mortenson, as well as Tony's wife, Helen, and daughter, Abby.

He gave them his name and phone number.

By his bedtime his eyes were drooping, he had covered an area about 40 miles away from shore along the Florida coast. The task seemed more daunting than he had first realized. There had to be a better way.

Later the next day, his dad got a call from the Miami Herald. "Mr. Benjamin?"

"That's right," he answered.

"I'm Brad Schofield, with the Miami Herald."

"Hello Mr. Schofield," Dan answered.

"We received an interesting email from you, I believe, with an attachment of a note that you claim could be from the NFL players lost at sea?" Mr. Schofield confirmed.

"I'm thinking it's authentic, Mr. Schofield. I have no reason to think it isn't. My son caught it drifting down the creek behind our house, with a casting net. What do you make of it?" Dan asked.

Mr. Schofield answered, "I can't tell. Not much to go on except they may be shipwrecked on an island somewhere off the eastern seaboard. If you let me get a little background info on you and your son, where you live and how you came to find this note, I think this would be a good human-interest story. We can see what kind of feedback we can get."

He put the phone on speaker and called Levi to sit for the interview. Levi told the reporter how old he was and where he went to school. He said they have a dock and he was shrimping when he saw a Coke bottle drifting toward his dock. He told the reporter that he keeps trash out of his part of the creek. He said he caught it with his shrimp net and when he got it in, he saw it had a note in it. It had gotten wet, but once it dried, it was pretty easy to read.

"What do you expect to do with it?" the reporter asked.

Levi went on to tell him how he had thought about using Google Earth to search the ocean for them, "but it could take a long time," he finished.

The reporter ended the interview and told Levi to pull up tomorrow's online paper. "Your story will be in there," he said. He thanked them both and said he would be in touch.

"Wow, we're going to be online," Levi said, excited by the thought.

The next day, Mr. Benjamin saw the story had gone out on Facebook, Twitter, Google, Reddit and even Pinterest. The headline read, "A True to Life Message in a Bottle was Found," and then the story went on about how now there is hope in finding the missing NFL players Maurice Munoz and Tony Mortensen along with his wife and daughter, the family who were reported lost at sea in June.

There were a lot of hits on the story and an overwhelming response to help. Levi saw the picture of the note and knew it was being seen around the world.

One interested local web page designer emailed him and offered to set up a page for him to help coordinate areas of the ocean to be searched and even asked him how close he suggested zooming in. Some folks volunteered for night watch to look for fires on islands. Levi found a map of Florida and the eastern seaboard and put it on the wall in his room and used a ruler to draw and label grids. He would assign a grid to all the new searchers and have them email him at what time and how long they spend looking in the assigned areas. He was serious now about seeing if his idea would actually work. Each searcher was represented by a different color pushpin. In the first three days after the website was posted on his Facebook page, over twenty searchers had signed up. After five days, another thirty. Levi continued to search and the map had pushpins in all the grids.

CHAPTER NINE

The next day, Abby was up early and wanted to see if Michael had come back. She did not hear from him all day yesterday and was worried that something bad might have happened. When she walked to the edge of the pool, she looked down into the water and saw the whitest boy she ever saw again, walking up behind her. She swirled around and laughed loudly at him. "I was going to scare you!" he said.

"I saw your reflection in the water," she laughed back. They were both happy to see each other.

"What happened to you yesterday? Where were you? I waited all day. What happened to my bottle?" Abby asked.

"Okay, I'll tell you. I'm getting to it," he said anxiously, like any kid she knew.

"Okay!" she said, and smiled a little.

Michael started his story, "I saw a little river running into an area with a lot of docks. I turned your bottle loose at the entrance of that creek and guided it with bursts of water to keep it in the current. I saw a boy with a net a few docks down so I pushed it toward him. I could see he wanted to catch it."

"Aaaah! Really?" Abby gasped.

"Yes and guess what?" Michael hesitated.

"Tell me! What happened?" Abby couldn't wait to hear.

"He caught it and carried it up to his house," Michael said and smiled at Abby. "He nearly caught the supership, too!" he added.

"Oh, Michael!" and she hugged his neck. Michael couldn't believe how warm her body was. He put his arms around her. "Thank you so much, Michael," she said as tears rolled down her cheek. They talked a while longer until he told her he had better get back home, he had been gone a long time. They decided to write notes in the sand at a hidden area off the path with a stick and to leave the stick sticking up if they had a message for the other.

As Abby walked back to camp, her whole demeanor changed. She passed a mango tree along the way and picked a ripe fruit to add to the dinner table. She walked along the beach thinking about Michael. Wow! She thought to herself. She knew no one she knew believed that aliens from another world were real. She had seen Independence Day and Star Wars but even she didn't really think that aliens existed. Now, she has met one.

She saw Maurice standing near some rocks at the water's edge filleting fish. He was cleaning a few of the larger fish he had caught with his rod and reel with his pocket knife. Abby saw that his fingers and hands were dark with tan and scratched up from all the sharp rocks and sharp fins. He had gotten better at catching fish along one area where large rocks stick up out of the water high enough to stand on. Since he could reach out above the deeper water there, he fabricated a fishing net out of a bed sheet. He used some of the plentiful sea urchins as bait. He would break a few sea urchins up and place them inside the middle of the spread-out sheet with a small rock to help sink the middle of it. The sides were lowered just below the surface by short ropes tied to each of the four corners. He would then slowly and evenly lift the sheet corners up out of the waters, catching small fish as they would attack the urchin meat. The supply of small fish was endless here. He saw Abby walking up behind him. "Hey, Abs!" he said, smiling her way.

"Hey Mo!" she said.

"You want to help me?" he asked.

"Sure," she offered eagerly to help.

"Okay, you stand up here beside me and hold these two lines, and when we get some fish in it, we're going to gently lift up the corners and bring them up out of the water," Maurice explained.

"Okay," she said. She wanted to talk to him about Michael but she couldn't. She patiently watched as the small fish started to swim over the edge of the sheet and began to nibble on the floating urchin pieces.

"You ready?" Maurice asked. She looked at him and nodded. "Now, slowly pull up on the lines at the same speed as me." She slowly lifted the heavy water-filled sheet as it began draining from small slits Maurice had cut it. There were six or seven small fish in it. "Great job," Maurice said, as he carried the draining sheet to a bucket he had sat down on the beach.

"Mo?" she began.

"Yes, Abs?" he answered.

"Do you believe in aliens?" she asked.

He looked at her. "Do I believe in aliens? No, I guess I have to say I've never seen a UFO or aliens from another planet," and asked right back, "Have you?"

She was caught off guard but didn't say anything. "I've never seen a UFO, either," she said sort of truthfully. "Why can't there be such things as aliens?" she asked.

Maurice paused to think about how to answer that. All he could think of was the standard, tried and true answer he knew. "In space, Abs, the distances are so great it would take many lifetimes to travel such distances. It's possible but not very."

"But, you think it is possible?" She went on.

"I'd be very surprised to meet one." He smiled at her and made a funny face. "Hi! I'm Carl! From Pluto!" he said. She laughed out loud.

"Nice to meet you, Carl!" she played along laughing at his silly face.

Maurice picked up the sheet and went to catch a few more fish for dinner. "Come help me. You bring me luck!" he said.

She said okay and went along.

Tony was with Helen on the boat resting out of the heat. At least on the water, a constant breeze blew through the windows and stirred the curtains. Their time together here on this island had bonded them together even more and Tony did his best to reassure her that he was doing everything he could think of to be ready if a ship or plane came by. He was certain their young family was going to make it off this island somehow. The joint efforts of Tony to protect and provide for their family and Helen's growing love for the most important people in her life caused her to do everything in her power to be supportive and helpful and to protect Abby. They held each other. Helen cried for her family as Tony pressed his cheek against her head and let her cry.

CHAPTER TEN

The next day, Michael met Abby again and took her on a ride to see a little more of Atlantis. They had to keep their rides short so she wouldn't be missed if someone came looking for her.

"So, what do you think we should do next to get someone to rescue us?" Abby asked as she rode along observing the ocean floor, which was not the ocean floor but a spaceship covered with ocean floor. "No wonder no one ever saw it, I'm looking at it and I still don't see it," Abby observed.

"Yeah, great isn't it?" Michael went on.

"We better get back." Abby said.

"Okay", he said as he turned back toward the small island and touched the dash in front of him. "Hold on!"

"I've been thinking about what I could do and there are some things I can think of. One is to let you know when a ship is coming this way so you can go start the fire signal," Michael said.

"That's a great idea!" Abby said. "Oh, Michael, I can't wait to get home."

Michael thought she was beautiful, especially when she smiled. He was mesmerized by her smile. He also liked her complexion. Her soft, warm, tanned skin was in sharp contrast to his. Abby was the first human he had ever seen up close and in person. He felt a sadness rush over him. He was going to miss her.

CHAPTER ELEVEN

The Miami Coast Guard was notified about the possibilities of the NFL members' status changing from being lost at sea to becoming possible castaways. The focus was now on islands throughout this part of the Atlantic.

Just three nights later, Levi was staring at an island on his screen and was about to move on when an email came in at 9:30 pm on a Friday night from Eliza Martinez. She was on the bulletin board map with her assigned area represented by a red pushpin. The note asked him to look at an area indicated by the attached picture of the area. Her note ended in three exclamation points. It was an island and if you zoomed in enough, it did look like the word "Help" was spelled out on its beach in tree trunks. He felt a chill start crawling across his back. He looked down and saw chill bumps on his arms that made the hairs on his arms stand up and felt like the hair on his head was trying to stand up, too. "Dad!"

CHAPTER TWELVE

Michael was in his supership when he spotted an ocean vessel on his radar. He stopped and drifted to the surface. He could see a ship. His first thought was to get to Abby. He submerged the supership and dropped to the bottom of the ocean, speeding off toward the island.

Aboard the Coast Guard vessel, Capt. Collevechio was watching the sky cloud up. The winds were picking up as well from a thunderstorm headed in his direction. The stronger winds were causing the already choppy surf and waves to get bigger, as his ship continued on to the preset coordinates leading him directly to the island spotted on Google Earth.

Unexpectedly, out here in the middle of nowhere, a radar blip was picked up momentarily then lost, found again and then it just disappeared. Capt. Collevechio was informed. He took position on the deck, scanning the ocean surface with binoculars. The unidentified vessel was last headed on coordinates close to their own. The captain knew there was an island out here because he had seen the image himself. He also saw the image with the HELP sign on the beach. This unidentified island had been amazingly spotted by searchers specifically looking for castaways. The captain knew that this island could very well have stranded boaters on it.

Through online satellite images, the island was shown to have all the requirements the searchers were looking for, including a HELP signal on the beach. Perhaps this could be where the football families had landed. The entire concept was groundbreaking.

But the radar hit told the experienced captain they were not alone. He thought at first perhaps there was a disabled ship drifting around out here somewhere. He steadied his body on a rail and raised his binoculars. Carefully and with intense focus, he started scanning from left to right, following the horizon as best he could as the ship bobbed up and down, sideways and every other way. He stopped as a large swell passed underneath the boat and had time to think, the way the water goes, so goes us. The target's direction was captured before it disappeared. It seemed to be headed in the same direction toward the island.

"That's different," he said to the chief petty officer, next to him.

"Sir?" the chief asked for clarification.

"The radar target just disappeared as it turned toward the same island where we're headed."

"Could it have been a sub, sir?" the XO asked. The captain pondered the question as he walked back toward the bridge. Where did it go was another question.

"Land ho!" one of Boatswain's mates called out.

Capt. Collevechio raised his binoculars again and could see the island in the distance as the ship moved up and over the waves with ease. He scanned around again. He was certain if there had been any ship out here other than a submarine, he would see it.

Michael let his supership drift up to the edge of the shore. He got out and was careful to make sure no one was around. He slipped into the forest. When he got to the pool, he didn't see Abby. He ducked back into the trees and headed toward Abby's camp. He crept up as close as he could until he spotted Abby with her mother preparing a meal. He picked up a small pebble and threw it at her. It missed but hit the table causing them both to look up.

"What was that?" Helen asked.

"I don't know," Abby said, but she looked in the direction from which the stone came and saw Michael's white hand wave to her. She told her mom she would be back in a minute. She walked around the area away from Michael and he came around to meet her in a heavy forested area. "A ship is coming!" He said, "Come with me!" They took off for the beach.

"Abby! Where are you going?" Helen called after her but she was gone.

"I have to tell Dad! He's on the boat!" she whispered excitedly. They ran down to the edge of the forest toward where the ship was headed. They could see it closing in. "You better get out of here!" Abby told Michael.

When she didn't hear him moving, she stopped and looked back at him. He was frozen, staring toward the beach with fear. The Coast Guard Ship was heading right for where he had left his supership. He knew if they hit it or even just get close to it, that they were going to find it. Michael just stood there.

"Michael! Hide in the woods!" Abby called to him.

He finally snapped out of his initial shock and looked at Abby. "Hide in the woods!" she said again. He turned and ran a few steps farther back, out of sight, stopped and turned around. He could see the ship continue in and it seemed like someone on board was looking right at him. He ducked down and took a few more steps even deeper back into the thicker foliage. He could still see a little. He saw Abby running toward the beach and waving her arms, yelling, "Here! Over here! Hey!" She continued to run down the beach until finally the boat veered off its direct course toward the supership to intercept her. Unfortunately, it didn't move far enough away for Michael to be able to get across the beach undetected, but it was far enough that the supership wasn't likely to get hit by the bigger ship now. "Way to go, Abby," Michael whispered.

Abby could see someone standing on the bow using binoculars to look up and down the beach and then back at her. Although the sophisticated radar of the Coast Guard vessel was continually sweeping the shoreline, it couldn't relocate the lost bogey. It looked like it went this direction and should be visible on radar but he could see nothing. Now he wasn't sure if what he was looking at was a huge ray or something else. He couldn't see any indication of anything on his radar at all. He turned his attention back toward the rescue. He saw the excited young lady running and yelling to get their attention. He guessed she was running toward the others here. The ship followed alongside in deeper water. The XO handed the captain the loudspeaker microphone. He put the mike near his mouth just as a sudden chill crept across him. He pushed the button. "This is Captain Collevechio, of the US Coast Guard. What is your name?!" he called out.

She stopped for a moment and looked his way. "Abby...Abby!" She was so nervous and shaken and out of breath, she could hardly speak. "Mortenson!" she finally was able to get out.

A cheer went up on the Coast Guard vessel. "How many others are there with you?" was his next question.

She thought about it. *Mom, Dad, Mo and me, and Michael, but I won't count him,* she smiled to herself. "Three!" she answered.

"Does anyone need medical attention?" was the last question from the captain before he cut the engine and dropped anchor in deeper water, still behind the supership. The crew was in the process of setting a smaller, more maneuverable boat onto the water.

"No! I don't think so!" she called back. *Dang,* Abby thought. Still not out of sight of Michael. She would have to think of something else.

The Coast Guard ship captain, Captain Collevechio, couldn't stop looking at the radar screen for the object that had looked so out of place in front of him. He was curious if this object was still around. As he was boarding the smaller boat, he continued sweeping the island in the direction they were headed. Farther along around the island, he spotted the cabin cruiser bobbing in the calm waters. He hailed the boat and announced their presence. "This is the US Coast Guard! Is anyone aboard," came from the larger boat.

Calls immediately came from the floating home. "Here! We're here!" came from Tony.

Maurice was standing on the deck after coming out of the engine compartment. "We're here!" he called. "Wooo hooo!" he yelled, "We're rescued! We're rescued!"

The small boat dropped anchor before it beached. The radar on the Coast Guard vessel that picked up the blip of a smaller vessel had lost that ping as it neared the island and now as it continued sweeping the area with constant surveillance, they saw nothing.

The larger rescue vessel had stopped less than 100 feet from the supership. Sentries were posted to keep a lookout. Michael was hiding as he watched the Coast Guard ship intently from his hiding place. He saw a smaller boat being lowered into the water and the captain and a couple of the crew all got in and were headed to shore. All but the captain had a smile on his face. The captain kept looking up and down the beach.

Abby's dad and Maurice ran out into the surf to meet them. During the excitement, Abby called to her mom, "I'll be right back!"

"Wait!" Helen called back. "Where're you going?" she asked.

"I have to do something! I'll be right back!" and she bolted from the camp area. She ran and ran. She ran through the forest faster than she had ever run before. She had to get far enough down the beach that she could get into the water without being seen. It was too risky for Michael to try.

Michael heard someone running behind him. He was frightened and stooped behind a thick bush. He followed the sounds and saw a figure near the forest line. He recognized Abby and saw her go into the water. He could also see the Coast Guard ship and a crew member on the deck. He was looking the other way when Abby made a break for the water. She took deep breaths and swam underwater most of the way. She came up once for air near the Coast Guard ship and found the supership not far away. She swam under the supership and got inside. Michael then saw a swirl of water as the supership silently slipped away from the shoreline. It continued away from shore smoothly and quietly, barely disturbing the water. No one noticed the small blip on the radar moving away from shore.

"Nice!" Michael smiled. Then he thought about how mad his mom was going to be.

Abby didn't know how she was going to find Atlantis without Michael, but she had to try. She looked at the radar and settings already programmed into the craft. The board in front of her had a home button on it. She pushed the button; the craft turned in the water and started moving forward. She saw a throttle control and pushed it forward like she had seen Michael do. The ship headed toward the surface. She pulled back but not before coming completely out of the water and skimming along the surface until it caught a wave and was underwater again.

Back on the Coast Guard ship, radar picked up the unidentified object heading away from the island.

Abby pulled back the throttle and let the ship settle back down toward the bottom.

"Captain?" yelled the XO to the smaller boat where the captain sat, headed toward the shore now, "I have a radar contact." Captain Collevechio stopped and looked out across the waves and saw nothing. He spoke to Tony for a moment and asked him if there were any other vessels around the island and if he had seen anything unusual. Tony hadn't seen a thing and didn't know what the captain was talking about. "I want to check something and I'll be back shortly. Please follow my crew's instructions and we will get you all back home today." the captain assured him. He smiled then made his way back to his command vessel. Tony and Maurice began stowing items so their boat could be towed.

CHAPTER THIRTEEN

With Abby at the controls, the craft began slowing down and then stopped exactly where they stopped before. She saw the outcropping where the door was. How do I get in? she wondered. "Hello there!" she called out from inside the supership. She remembered he said there was a way to open it from inside the ship. She decided she would try the obvious one. There was another button that seemed to be apart from the rest. She pushed it and it worked. A door large enough to drive into opened into a large chamber. She steered the supership inside, and once inside, the door behind her closed and the water level began to come down. The blip on the Coast Guard's radar disappeared again. She opened the door and crawled out to a female being just as white as Michael, only taller. "Hello!" Abby said, hoping that she spoke English.

The being stood there looking at her quizzically, wearing a black dress. Abby quickly said, "I know you can speak English. Michael told me. He's in trouble and needs your help."

"Where is Michael?" A high-pitched voice came from the being. "He's on the island, hiding!" Abby explained. "We need to get him off before someone finds him! There are people there now who came to rescue us. If they find him, he'll be afraid. I don't know what will happen. Please! We have to go get him." She was out of breath.

The female took Abby by the hand. "Okay," she said. "Come with me."

"Where are we going? We need to get Michael!" Abby kept stressing.

"We will," the extremely white lady said. Then the doors opened in front of her. She took two steps and stopped.

All of a sudden, Abby walked out onto a catwalk that circled above a room of activity. The area below was sectioned off with the same white-skinned beings as Michael, in regular assorted clothing, looking and working like any office or factory Abby could imagine, with various products sitting around. Abby saw a bag of tortilla chips sitting on a table and asked if she could have some. They gave her a bag and a Mountain Dew soft drink. She ate chips and drank two sodas as she walked around the area. She met at least a dozen of these alien earthlings. They were nice, they were all smiling and each looked a little different from each other. The woman told Abby her name was Fjur, and yes, she was Michael's mother. They went into another room where men in uniforms were sitting. They all stood when Fjur walked into the room with Abby.

"Fjur! What's going on?" One extremely ghostly looking male stood up and looked directly at Abby with a look of fear.

"We have to go get Michael," Fjur told them. "He is at the island now and there are people there who may find him. You have to send someone after him." Fjur looked more upset now. "This is Abby," she said as the others stared at her and with their eyes about to pop out. Abby stared back. "She is Michael's friend. She's here to help us."

Abby stood in front of four other beings and began talking. "I met Michael on the island about ten miles away from here, and drove his supership here."

They looked at each other and a strange expression came over their faces like a smile. Michael was the only one who called the craft a supership. "We'll help," one of them said.

She said she just needed someone to take her back and get Michael out of there. "I think I know where he might be. I'll find him and send him to you."

"I'll go," volunteered a young adult male. "Me too," said another. One more volunteer made it three.

They led Abby through a large open atrium area with many of

the unusual white looking Alien Earthlings, or Alien Americans. She wasn't sure what to call them. *This is incredible*, she was thinking as she walked down long corridors with mall-sized areas with shops filled with things they would need. She saw many products she recognized. "Where did all this stuff come from?" she asked.

"We have help," Fjur said. Abby could tell Fjur was reluctant to share much information. They made their way to a different section of the craft that held a large hangar. Other crafts like the one Michael used were lined up. She thought there must have been a hundred. They made their way to a station and signed out three vehicles. "I'm Jay," the one leading her said.

"I'm Abby."

"It's nice to meet you, Abby. My friends here are Hopper and Bory. I think I know the island Michael goes to. Where is he?"

Abby began to explain how a rescue boat pulled up to the beach right next to the supership. "Michael couldn't get to it so I did and came here for help."

"Okay, we'll go get him," Jay said.

"I was able to get to it without being seen," Abby explained.

"Oh, you were seen," Jay said. "There's a big ship above us right now."

Abby suddenly felt the blood drain from her face. "Oh no, what have I done?" she cried.

"It's okay. They have no idea we are right under them," Bory added.

They headed toward the closest supership and up a short ladder to enter the elevated vessels from underneath. "Do you mind if I drive this time?" Jay looked at her and smiled a super white smile.

Abby smiled back and said, "If you want to."

They both got seated and buckled in. All three of these boys had been going out together since they were kids. All of them were born here and knew as much as any kid in high school and college. All three ships aligned themselves in a row to exit the hangar. Up ahead, a ramp going down into a large pool was manned by workers.

An all clear indicated by one of the workers assured them the tracks were unobstructed and the three ships could proceed down into the watery exit safely.

As soon as the third ship had exited the larger ship, the three super ships assumed a triangular formation with Abby and Jay at the point. Jay turned the ship toward the island and hit his communication button. "Is everybody ready?" Affirmative answers signaled they were ready to go. Jay had given instructions to distract the Coast Guard vessel by going in three directions, east, northeast and southeast. He and Abby would go southeast last after the cutter committed to one of the other directions. Then they would circle back and go get Michael.

Aboard the Coast Guard vessel, a ping could be heard from the radar detector. "Captain, we have an unidentified vessel just popping up on screen," the radar operator reported. The blip was coming into view on the scanner, no more than a thousand yards away. "Two objects now heading due east." The captain couldn't ignore the unidentified objects and ordered the coordinates to be set and headed at full speed to intercept the vessels on the screen. Then the objects separated by 45 degrees and continued on, picking up speed. Capt. Collevechio watched closely as the objects sped away. He was unable to keep up. After ten minutes, he ordered his ship to come about, having missed the third ship that had slipped out low, just above the ocean floor, undetected by his radar. He turned his ship back toward the island to resume his rescue mission.

CHAPTER FOURTEEN

As they neared the island but still far enough away so as not to be seen by those on shore, the three superships came to a halt. Abby told Jay she would find Michael and send him there. She thanked him and said it was nice to meet him. Jay smiled and opened the hatch so she could disembark. "I'll be right here," he said.

Abby looked around before coming completely out of the water. After seeing no one else, she made it to the woods. She ran toward where she last saw Michael. He was hiding in thick foliage and saw her as she approached. "Over here!" he whispered loudly. Abby ran to him. "Where have you been?" he asked.

"I went to get help!" she said. "Jay is in the supership near the rocks on the other side of the island where Maurice likes to fish."

"Jay? Jay's here?"

"Yes, and he's waiting for you. Get going, I have to get back to my family." Michael jumped up and headed to the rendezvous spot.

Abby ran back to the area where everyone was still moving things from the shore to the cabin cruiser. "Where have you been? Why are you wet?" Helen asked her.

"I was looking for something I lost," Abby said. "What?" Helen asked. "Oh, never mind, it's not important," Abby finished. Helen did not have time to press her further right then but decided she would ask her later.

A flurry of activity continued as Abby saw the Coast Guard

cutter coming into sight. It was nearing the area where everyone was working to prepare to leave the island.

Dad and the Coast Guard crew were preparing to tow his boat back to the mainland after the crew mechanic was still unable to get the motor going. The captain pulled the cutter closer to the cabin cruiser and after a short discussion, agreed to the tow. The towline was attached to the disabled vessel. Tony, Helen and Abby wanted to stay on the cabin cruiser and Maurice would ride on the cutter. After everything was stowed away, the cutter radioed in his coordinates and slowly moved ahead to tighten the towline carefully. The journey began.

Michael, in the meantime, had found the supership and boarded it. "You're in big trouble," Jay told Michael.

"Oh, shut up, I am not," he argued back with his older brother. "Let me drive!" Michael demanded.

"Oh no, put your seat belt on. We're going home," Jay said sternly, like big brothers do. "We need to wait until the Coast Guard starts moving so they don't see us." He backed the supership out from shore and slowly started around the island until they could see the activity ahead. They could tell that everything was ready and the crew was stowing the smaller boat and securing it to the larger one. Michael could see Abby darting in and out of sight, helping get things packed on the cabin cruiser. They saw the cutter moving out to sea and the cabin cruiser starting to move. Michael was feeling like he had lost his best friend. He felt like crying but never in a million years would he cry in front of Jay. Jay saw the look in his eyes though as Michael couldn't take his eyes off Abby. He sat there without saying a word to his little brother.

Finally, he couldn't resist any longer, like brothers behave all over the universe. "Did you say goodbye to your girlfriend?" Jay asked, trying not to smile.

Michael hit him hard on his thigh. "Shut up!" he said and turned back to watching the boats move away.

Jay waited twenty minutes before leaving his spot at the island. He was not willing to take a chance on being seen at this point.

On board the cutter, the captain was getting updates from the weather station. Winds were picking up with gusts up to tropical storm levels. He wanted to get the family back safely to Florida. He had placed a portable radio on board with Tony to maintain contact. He felt if they could maintain their speed, they would just make it ahead of the storm, but strong wind gusts had picked up earlier than expected and slowed their progress. The choppy waves became bigger. The cutter tried to turn into the wind when he could but with the nearly nine-ton cabin cruiser in tow, the cutter was slower than he anticipated. Each time the cutter crested these large swells and then dipped on the other side, the strain on the line would take its toll and began stretching the nylon rope.

About 45 minutes out from the island, the cutter surged forward as the rope holding the cruiser was pulled beyond its capacity. It was designed to hold twice this weight but this time the force of the ocean wave snapped the taut rope as the ocean flexed its watery muscles. It snapped and recoiled forcefully.

The sudden jerk caused a jolt aboard the cruiser and it listed uncontrollably starboard. Helen was moving across the aft section when she was carried by her weight and momentum right over the railing. Abby screamed, "Mom!" Tony was carried to the starboard bulkhead and lost his footing as well. Abby was holding as tight as she could to the railing. Once she saw her mom topple over the side, she ran across the deck, grabbed a circular life preserver and jumped overboard to find her mom whom she could no longer see. This time, there had been nothing to grab hold of as she toppled over the aft railing of the cabin cruiser.

The choppy ocean waves began to obscure Tony's vision. Tony looked for Abby. She was also gone. He got to his feet and grabbed the radio. "Mayday, mayday, Helen and Abby both fell overboard! Mayday, mayday!"

The response was immediate. "We copy and are turning around,"

XO's voice called back to him. Tony was adrift and Helen and Abby both were in the water. He was unsure of what to do. He tried to steer the vessel but had no control. He was again at the mercy of the waves. The crew member observing the tow immediately relayed to the captain that the rope had snapped and they had lost the boat.

Tony yelled toward the ocean as loud as he could, "Helen! Abby!" as he stood at the rails, scanning the ocean for the sight of his wife and daughter. The waves made it nearly impossible to spot them. At one point he saw a life preserver but no one was on it. Tony just knew they were gone. It was impossible to find them in this water. His heart sank.

Helen was out of sight. She had gulped a mouth full of seawater and was choking and snorting the burning saltwater. Abby had leaped out of the boat to find her mom. Helen couldn't see the life preserver; she was underwater and swam hard toward the surface but couldn't make progress. *Where is the surface,* she remembered thinking before the last of her oxygen was being used up. She knew she couldn't hold her breath any longer. She thought one last time of the picture of them all together at home that was sitting on her bookcase. She remembered thinking that she was going to miss everybody so much. She began crying as the last of her breath was gone and she was at that point of giving up. Her consciousness was leaving her. She was going down.

Then all of a sudden, just when all her strength was gone, when she couldn't finish her last prayer and began to sink, she felt something beneath her drifting legs, pushing her up. She opened her eyes but could only see a blur. She still had not tried to breathe. A surge of pure determination and willpower gave her one last boost of energy. Something large, flat, hard and shiny was lifting her out of the water. She was stunned momentarily thinking it was a shark. Then, out of the depths, virtually out of nowhere, she was lifted out of the water. She gasped and blew out the water in her sinuses and burning throat.

Abby popped up beside her, "Mom, Mom! Are you okay?"

Helen coughed and spit and snorted and blew out the remaining salty water that burned her sinuses and made her eyes watery. In the bright sunshine, she could barely make out shapes but she recognized this one immediately. "Abby! Oh, Abby! Where did you come from?" She hugged her daughter with all her might.

"Mom, I thought I wasn't going to find you!" Abby yelled.

"What is this we're sitting on?" Helen asked.

"Oh, Mom, It's a secret supership! I'll tell you later." Then, another head came up out of the blue water and this one was unbelievable. "Hold on, Mom. This is Michael. He's not from another planet, he was born here. He's an American citizen. He lives out here. I'll tell you more about him later. Mom? He can't stay but I wanted you to meet him. He helped us get rescued. I knew we were going to get rescued," Abby tried to explain.

Helen was still staring at the white-skinned boy. "It's nice to meet you, Michael. Thank you for helping us."

"You're welcome. I'm glad you get to go home," he said and smiled at Abby.

"I better go. Sorry to leave you swimming but I'll be close if you need me," Michael said to Abby.

"It's nice to meet you, too, Mrs. Mortenson. I'll be watching football games from now on," he added.

"Goodbye, Michael," Helen said.

"What did you say we were sitting on?" Helen asked again.

Abby looked up to see the Coast Guard ship closing in on them. Michael smiled big. "You're about to go home," he said.

"Oh, Michael," Abby said and hugged his cool, wet neck, "I'm never going to forget you, Michael."

"I'm not ever going to forget you either," he said. Helen watched the embrace and knew this was something she would never talk about with anyone else.

"Wait!" Abby said. "I have an idea. Meet me at the dock of the boy who found the note in one month from today. Maybe he could meet you, too!"

Before he left, he swam over and grabbed a life preserver floating a short distance away. He handed it to Abby. As she held the other side of it, she looked at Michael. He looked a little sad, she thought. "Bye, Abby," he said as he turned and went back under the supership.

"Bye, Michael!" The supership gently sank beneath them, leaving them treading water and holding on to the life preserver.

He had heard the ship closing in. On board, the captain was blinking his eyes against the constantly bobbing binoculars, thinking they must be blurred to see three heads bobbing up above the waves.

"He's such a nice boy," Helen said, staring into the water where Michael just disappeared.

Abby smiled at her mom as they held onto the life preserver. "Here we go," Abby said. They treaded water as the Coast Guard ship closed the last 200 feet. The radar man continued to pick up radar hits right in their position but they saw nothing, scanning the ocean. "Hey!" Helen waved as three life preservers hit the water around them.

"Where's the third person?" he called down.

Abby looked at her mom. Helen smiled at her and said, "There are just two of us!"

A safe distance away and bobbing up and down in the ocean waves, Michael saw the outline of the U.S. Coast Guard ship slowly approach them. He took one last look and disappeared underwater.

Aboard the Coast Guard vessel, Maurice rode shotgun with the captain and the XO on the bridge. Tony was drifting on the cabin cruiser but in sight of the cutter.

On the approach to the people in the water, Maurice heard the radar man like everyone else. He looked toward the XO and the captain, who were looking at each other in stunned silence. "An unidentified bogey spotted coming from a westerly heading, traveling at a high rate of speed, sir." Captain Collevechio picked up his binoculars for the third time and scanned the horizon again from the port side.

"Captain, the object stopped. It's stopped" announced the radar man.

"Captain, what do you make of the radar contact?" the XO asked.

"I don't know," the concerned captain stated flatly. He turned to Maurice. "Mr. Munoz, do you know who might be moving around out there?"

"No," Maurice answered, stunned by all of this. "We haven't seen a soul since we've been here." He shook his head. "More rescuers?" He finally made a guess.

"I don't think so," the captain went on. The captain radioed to Tony that he had Helen and Abby both in his sights and they were both okay.

"Thank God! And thank you," Tony told the captain over the radio. He was much relieved to finally know they were both safe.

"Yes, sir," the captain replied. He told Tony he would be back for him straight away after bringing those two aboard. The Coast Guard crew pulled Helen and Abby on board. And after replacing the tow line with a heavier rope, the captain regained his positioning and continued on to collect the drifting cruiser with a distraught captain of its own on board. Tony cried in the arms of his wife and daughter.

The Coast Guard cutter resumed its heading to Mayport, Florida with the grateful family again in tow. After a while, Abby called out in her playground scream, "I see land!" The ship's chief asked Maurice what his first big meal was going to be. He hesitated for a moment in deep thought. "A juicy NY strip steak still sizzling as it is brought to the table from The Capital Grill in Miami. It's got to be thick with ground peppercorns and a bottle of a nice dry red wine. For dessert, I'd like a big slice of Black Forest cake from my favorite German restaurant there."

"That sounds great," added the XO, "except we're taking you to Mayport."

"Okay, it doesn't matter. What's the best steakhouse in Jacksonville, then?" he asked the XO.

"Well, Just so happens, I believe there's a Capital Grill in Jacksonville," he said. "I've been to it. Good choice." Then as they both turned their attention back on the voyage, Maurice walked back and waved at Tony from the stern of the larger ship. He was making his way back, trying to walk steadily across the constantly moving deck when he heard the radar man again.

"Three bogeys at our six, sir, at a distance of three thousand feet, Captain."

"What's their heading?" asked the captain.

"Same as ours, Captain. Looks like they are separating in a line three across and holding steady."

The captain thoughtfully looked at the XO. "We can't let them come upon the back of our vessel in tow."

"They have stopped, sir," the radar man announced as the XO observed the craft.

The captain was contemplating giving chase but after this family's ordeal, he decided to let it go. "Continue on course," was the order.

The captain had radioed ahead their estimated time of arrival to the port in Mayport. Anticipation was high, family members had been notified and were all congregating at the dock. A crowd exceeding three hundred was waiting for them. Family, friends and fans, plus cable TV anchors and newspaper people all were waiting there. Excitement and tears of joy were abundant as the 66-foot Coast Guard cutter was spotted and made its way to the dock with the now famous cabin cruiser in tow. Everyone was cheering and waving to them.

The castaways were overwhelmed with emotion as they disembarked their vessels. Maurice and Tony both had beards and had lost an extreme amount of weight, Helen was thin and sunburned but smiling and happy to be back. Abby was the star after her mother told them of how she had leaped into the water with a life preserver to rescue her when she fell off the boat. They were front page news. The captain and crew also had their pictures taken for front page news stories and were also called heroes.

Famous football players and coaches from the Miami Dolphins, Jacksonville Jaguars and Baltimore Ravens all were there. Tony and Helen's parents were there to see them and their granddaughter. Hugs and tears, cheers and welcome home signs from fans were scattered throughout the crowd. Everyone was excited and happy for the rescued family. Maurice's wife jumped in his arms, immediately noticing his weight loss and telling him she liked the beard and hugged him hard.

Standing in the middle of the crowd was a little boy with his daddy. Abby remembered Michael's description of the boy on the dock with the casting net. He slowly began walking toward the rescued castaways. Also with him, whom Abby did not know, was a young lady. The three of them stood together.

Captain Collevechio turned toward the rescued family and said, "There are some folks here who want to meet you. I think the young man who found the message in the bottle is right over there." He pointed to the Benjamin's who were standing quietly in the crowd. The three adults looked at each other for a clue about what he was talking about. They walked up to meet them.

"This is Levi Benjamin and his father, Dan. Levi found the message in the bottle and this little lady is the one who found the island you were on, Eliza Martinez."

"Nice to meet you," she said.

The rescued party looked at one another. The adults were confused and astounded. "Message in a bottle?" asked Tony as he looked at the others. "Who put a message in a bottle?"

Abby had wanted to meet Levi. Dan could see Levi, his little genius, was embarrassed to meet her and couldn't form a thought to create a sentence.

"Thank you," Abby said.

Levi was speechless. He finally managed to say in almost a whisper, "You're welcome," as if he were addressing an adult. His dad had to lean forward to hear him say it.

"Invite her over," Levi heard his dad say.

"Wanna come over?" he blurted out before he realized what he was saying. "Sure!" was the quick reply. "Let me ask my mom."

"Okay," Levi was stuck again.

A couple of breaths later, "When?" came the next question that caused Levi to blush and get stuck again.

"Just a minute," as he looked at his dad and asked, "When, Dad?"

"I know they live in Maryland now, so just tell them to give me a call a day or so before they plan to come," Dan finished with the invitation clearly offered and he and Levi backed up and let Eliza step forward to say hello.

"It is so awesome to meet you," Eliza said excitedly.

Capt. Collevechio continued the introductions. "And Eliza here was the person who first spotted the island where we found you on Google Earth."

"What?" Tony asked, totally flabbergasted. He, Abby and Maurice looked at each other.

"I didn't even know you could do that!" Maurice exclaimed and reached out his hand to her. She relaxed a little and smiled at the much larger, disheveled-looking man. "Thank you," he said with all sincerity. Thank you also came from the others as they all surrounded the young lady.

"How did you do that?" Tony asked.

"Levi showed me how," she said.

"So, how did you do this?" Tony asked Levi.

Levi decided this was a question he could answer. "I was looking at the stars on the map."

"The stars," Abby exclaimed. "I felt so dumb for drawing those!"

All the adults looked at Abby. "Oh, no, that was a great idea!" he retorted.

"I didn't think it was," she said again.

"It was though," he insisted. They looked at each other for a moment and suddenly both started laughing.

Maurice was the first to find words. "Abs, you put a message in a bottle and threw it out into the water there? And it came all the way over here? Why didn't you tell anybody?"

She looked at him and the others, knowing they were waiting for an answer. "I don't know," she said, and turned back to her Dad. "Levi asked if we can come visit him. Can we?" she asked her dad.

"Of course, sweetheart," Tony answered.

After a while, they said goodbye to each other. They talked to the crowd and thanked everyone for their prayers and efforts to find them. He thanked Capt. Collevechio and the crew who came to rescue them and again thanked the Benjamins and Eliza. He told his teammates he would be back joining them as soon as he could and thanked them for showing up today. He and Maurice waved their goodbyes to the crowd and said they were going to get something to eat besides fish tonight. A laugh from the crowd and they began to disperse. The tired family headed to the nearest hotel to get cleaned up and ready for their favorite meals with their parents.

At dinner, as Tony was about to take his first bite of good old steak, he looked at Abby. "Abby?" he called to get her attention. "You are amazing! You saved us! You saved your mom, too! I just can't tell you how proud we all are of you."

The other adults around the table were looking at her and beaming with pride for their little hero. Maurice raised his glass, "We have a little thing we do for heroes. Get your glasses, everyone." They all raised their wine glasses to Abby and said in unison, "Hip, hip hooray! Hip, hip hooray," and by the third hip, hip hooray, all the patrons in the restaurant had joined in. "Hip, hip hooray!" came from everyone in the room. Abby smiled even though she was a little embarrassed.

The next day, Tony and Maurice went to the marina and found a mechanic that would take the cabin cruiser in for repairs and left it there.

Tony, Helen and Abby borrowed their parent's car and continued on to Baltimore where they were meeting a realtor and beginning the search for their new home. Maurice rode with his wife back toward

Miami. They planned to stop along the way to break up the trip and spend time alone together before going back home.

CHAPTER FIFTEEN

Abby talked to Levi on the phone and planned to visit him one month after the rescue. It was all set and on that day, exactly one month later, she and her mother arrived at the Benjamin's at 11:00 am.

After saying hello at the door, Dan told Abby that Levi was in his room. "He's been waiting for you." He pointed to Levi's room and told her to go on back. "Surprise him," he said. He invited Helen into the kitchen for a cup of coffee while Abby walked back to his room.

She stopped at his partially opened door. She had spent a lot of time thinking about what she was going to say at this moment. She still wasn't sure. She liked him though and thought he was smart. She had already made up her mind about that. Maybe it was how diligently he pursued them or how clever he was to figure out how to find someone who was castaway on an island or how much of a hero he had become.

When she got to his room with the fake crime scene tape on his door, she saw him as he sat at his computer with his back to the door playing a video game. Standing there looking at him, she suddenly just loved him. She wanted to talk to him. Maybe she wanted to introduce him to Michael, but she felt like she should talk to him first and see what he was like. The determination and intensity he focused on the screen didn't really surprise her. *All boys do that*, she thought and smiled. "Levi?"

He turned around and saw Abby standing there beaming a huge

smile at him. He couldn't help himself and smiled big back as he waved hi from his chair

She went in and he invited her to sit beside him at the computer. "What cha doing?" she asked.

"I'm just playing a game," he said back.

"Oh!" she said.

"How do you like Baltimore?" he asked, although he had never been.

"It's okay," she said. "Everyone is nice."

After a moment, he jumped up. "Hey, I've got something to show you." He got up and went to a shelf. When he came back, she saw him holding a bottle that she recognized instantly. She felt a wave rush over her. What had they done with this little Coke bottle? It was a major part of her story. At first she thought the idea of putting a note in a bottle was silly. Then it happened, something unbelievable happened, something so unbelievable happened that she can't tell anybody. Of course she could never tell her dad how she managed to get a Coke bottle over that long distance so fast. She would tell her mom since she had already met Michael and make her promise not to tell anyone else. She had thought about saying she tied it to the tail of a seagull that accidentally flew into another one during one of their frequent exhibitions of their aerial ballet skills. A mid-air collision caused one of them to get knocked out. She ran over, caught him and after seeing he was okay to fly, she decided she would tie the bottle with the note in it to his leg. Then she could say, "It must have fallen off close to Levi's house." So far, no one has even asked her.

Levi handed her the bottle. Abby stared at it for a few seconds before reaching for it. It suddenly hit her how all this started with this bottle and a little note a long way from here. Maybe it started when she made that wish on the shooting star. Abby wondered but she was unsure if that was the moment the magic happened. She knew one thing for sure, every time she saw a shooting star from now on, she would make a very important wish.

He began to tell her how he was fishing when he saw this bottle coming toward him in the current and how he used his casting net to catch it. He told her how he had to dry out the note because it was wet and hard to read at first. He told her how he was sitting out on the dock one night and wondered if they both might be looking at the constellations at the same time.

"Like in the movie, Fievel?" she asked. She stopped for a few seconds to try to remember the song the two mice sang to each other while in different places but both looking at the moon at the same time. She remembered thinking at that moment, she really did like him. That's when she finally and for real decided what she was going to do next.

"Yeah, I guess so," he replied, a little embarrassed.

Abby wanted to know all about the search for the island and she wanted to try it and see if she could see what they saw and if she would be able to recognize it. Levi sat down at his computer and Abby sat in a chair next to him. He opened the files and Google Earth. After positioning the mouse for the best position, Levi moved the mouse around and zoomed in on the lost island. She could easily see the island on the screen. Dad and Maurice had come pretty close to getting the shape right. She also saw an opening in the trees around the pool. A sunlight glare off the water made it easy to see from this direction. Then she saw another flash, what she thought was the glare of sunlight off something shiny, but it wasn't. "Aaah!" she gasped. It was Michael's white head and it was extremely white and looked out of place.

"What's the matter?" Levi asked when she seemed surprised to see something.

"Nothing," she quickly moved on to where the big HELP sign was on the beach. They moved those logs so no one would think someone was still there. As she zoomed in, she noticed she could see where the boat was and almost see the campsite and the hill where Dad had put a flag sheet. It is gone now. They took it down before they left. "This is amazing!" she said. "I can see everything!"

She looked at the time on his computer screen. "Hey?" she suddenly asked. "You said you caught this in a net?"

"Yes!" he said with pride.

"Can you show me how to throw a net?" she asked excitedly.

"Sure!" They jumped up and ran past the adults in the kitchen.

"We're going to the dock!" Levi called to his dad as they ran past. When they got outside, Levi called, "Blackie! C'mon!"

"You have a dog?" Abby asked.

"No," he replied. Then a small black cat swiftly, but with hardly a sound, whisked by the two of them like it was a race. "Your cat comes when you call him?"

"Yeah, he likes to go fishing," Levi answered.

As they got down to the end of the dock, the tide was nearly high and coming in quickly.

"Levi?" Abby called as she anxiously gathered her nerves to tell Levi why she was really here.

"What?" he asked.

"Can you keep a secret?" she started.

He looked suspiciously at her. "Yes," he answered carefully.

"Levi, do you believe that someone from another planet far away could come here?"

"I don't know. I guess," he said.

"Levi, I met someone on the island who came here from another planet long ago. He was our age. He was very white and very smart."

Levi couldn't stop looking at her. "Really?" he asked.

"Yes," she continued on. "He brought this bottle to you close enough for you to catch it."

Levi looked at her, amazed by what she was saying. "I asked him to meet us here today, one month from the day we were rescued." She looked out at the rushing tidal waters and thought she saw a shadow with water rushing around it leaving a little wake.

"Is he here...now?" Levi asked, looking up the creek.

"I think so," then Abby waved her hand toward the shadow and motioned for it to come over.

Michael was there. He had been waiting there since nine o'clock that morning. He was so excited that he couldn't sleep last night and had gotten up early to be here. He didn't want to take the chance of missing Abby. He was in the supership just under the surface. He had set his supership into a holding position through GPS and propulsion to give the illusion of hovering underwater. The top of the supership came up to the surface and Michael waved to Abby. Levi's mouth fell open. He stood there frozen.

"That's Michael, Levi. Wave to him," Abby said.

Levi raised his hand and gave a little wave with his mouth open and his eyes staring in awe at what he was seeing. Michael made sure his supership was set and slipped out from underneath the vessel. His white head popped up out of the water and he climbed up onto the floating dock. Abby helped him up as Levi watched in disbelief. They all stood together on the dock.

"Levi, this is Michael. He's not an alien, he was born on Earth. We think he's an American, too. Michael, this is Levi!"

"Hello, Levi," Michael smiled. Levi smiled back.

"I didn't know if you were going to catch that bottle. I didn't know what I was going to do if you missed it," Michael said. Levi asked if he was there then. "Yeah, and you almost caught me in your net," he added. Levi remembered feeling something heavy when he started to pull the net in.

"Ha!" Levi said. "I nearly caught that thing?" he pointed to the craft.

"That's Michael's supership!" Abby exclaimed. "It can go very fast and it can fly. I even drove it one time," she added.

"She sure did," Michael confirmed. "How did you find them so fast?" Michael asked.

"I used Google Earth and I had a lot of help," Levi explained.

"You should see it on his computer, Michael. He could zoom in right over the island. I think I even saw you there," Abby said.

He looked at her, "Really?"

"Yeah, your head was so shiny and bright, I think I saw it," she said, smiling.

"Levi, can I come visit you sometime?" Michael asked.

"Yeah, sure," he answered. "I come down here after school almost every day."

"You have to take him for a ride in your supership," Abby said.

"Okay," Michael agreed.

"Levi!" his dad called from his back porch.

"Uh oh, we better get going," Abby said.

Michael eased back in the water. "Come back Saturday, Michael, about this time and maybe we can talk some more," Levi said.

"Okay," Michael agreed. Then he looked at Abby. "Goodbye, Abby," he said.

"Goodbye, Michael. We'll figure out how to keep in touch," she added, and that made him feel better as he slipped under the water back to his supership.

Abby and Levi ran back up to the house to meet Mr. Benjamin and Helen, who were standing on the back patio. "We should be going, Abby." Mrs. Mortenson said.

"Okay," Abby answered back. "It was fun seeing you again Levi," Abby said.

Levi smiled and shook his head in agreement. They all said goodbye and Abby and her mom left to go back to their new home in Maryland. Abby waved goodbye to Levi from the car.

The online headline was, "The Bermuda Triangle was no match for NFL players Mortensen, Munoz and family members lost at sea." It told all about the incredible odds of finding the castaways and how finding a needle in a haystack would have been easier. That's the kind of odds that were beaten to find them. It told how they had been listed as the most current victims of the Bermuda Triangle and went on to tell stories of ships and planes lost there and never seen again.

Abby read the story of how Levi Benjamin had found a message in a bottle from Abby Mortensen and the idea he had to use Google Earth to search the ocean for the island where the castaways were believed to be stranded. It told about how the idea expanded to a web page for others who wanted to help. It told how Eliza Martinez spotted the white sheet flag on the hill and then the HELP sign on the beach. It included how over 100 searchers had eventually registered on a website to join in the search and pick a part of the ocean to search and explore. When Abby had finished reading the story of how they were rescued, she was astounded.

A few weeks later, Dan Benjamin got a call from Mr. Tony Mortenson himself, currently the most famous NFL player in the world, with the extraordinary online story of the giant wave that scuttled their boat far out at sea, exceeding 2 million hits. The unexpected call came through on his cell phone one afternoon. Normally, this time of day, no one he knew would be calling. Dan thought it was most likely some telemarketer. He usually would at least wait to hear if there was someone on the line, or a recording telling him his car warranty was about to expire and for him to hold on and a representative would be with him shortly, before he would hang up, but this time he was speechless.

"Mr. Benjamin?" Tony Mortenson asked.

"Yes," he answered.

"This is Tony Mortenson," Dan managed to not hang up. Tony expressed his heartfelt gratitude again for all the efforts he and Levi put into finding them.

"Yes, sir," Dan managed to squeak out.

Tony smiled on the other end of the phone. "The reason I called is to ask you if you and Levi can come up for a visit with us on the weekend before Christmas when we play Miami. The team and I would like to do something for you and the others who helped to find us," he went on. "We have airline, hotel and game tickets for you and your family if you'd like to come?"

"That sounds great but it's really not necessary Mr. Mortenson."

"Call me Tony. I know that, Dan but I need your help with something. I want to do this for the kids and the two teams will sponsor it. I'm extending the invitation to all those who participated in looking for us. We are going to invite them all onto the field for a special thanks from the NFL Commissioner and the mayor. I need your help in contacting them. I was hoping that Levi had a contact list."

"I believe he does," Dan confirmed. "I'll have him send you the list," Dan said.

"That would be great, Dan," Tony said and finished the call after getting Dan to accept a personal invitation to their new home.

CHAPTER SIXTEEN

The next Saturday at 9 am, Levi was sitting on the dock with Blackie to see if Michael would show up. The tide was coming in quickly and the water would soon be deep enough for the supership to easily maneuver down the creek. Levi unexpectedly happened to look up at the right time and was sure he saw it surface a few feet out and come to a stop. He gave a little wave but he couldn't see anything. In a few seconds a little white head popped out of the water with a big grin on it.

"Hey, Michael," Levi called.

"Hey, Levi," Michael called back as he swam up to the dock.

Levi told Michael it was safe to come on the dock that his dad wasn't home and would be gone for a little while.

Michael said that would be great but added, "But I need your help to do something first."

"Sure," Levi responded without hesitation like buddies do. The two boys already trusted each other so Michael explained what he saw. "There's a dolphin trapped on a sandbar a little way from here and it'll probably be another hour before the tide comes in far enough that he can get loose. I don't think he's going to make it that long. He doesn't look so good right now," Michael finished.

"Yeah," Levi yelled, "I'll help. Let me leave a note for Dad." He jumped up and ran to the house to leave a note.

While he was gone Michael looked around the backyard at the places he only saw from a distance. The swimming pool he thought was a funny idea. They have the ocean right here and they wanted a swimming pool. He could smell the chlorine in the water. He reached in and scooped up a handful of water and smelled it then emptied it back into the pool. He wanted to get in it sometime but right now they had an emergency to deal with. He saw Levi's cat, Blackie, at the end of the dock probably waiting for someone to come throw the shrimp net and catch him a snack.

Michael headed back toward the dock and called Blackie. "Here, Blackie. C'mon Kitty, kitty, kitty, kitty," he called. Blackie came right up to Michael's hand and rubbed his head and body against it. "Oh, you're so soft," Michael said softly and rubbed Blackie's head some more. He heard the back door slam and saw Levi running across the back yard towards the dock.

When Levi saw Blackie he said, "Hey, Blackie are you hungry?" He turned toward Michael and said, "Give me a second. Let me catch Blackie a few shrimp or a fish or something, Okay?" "Okay," Michael said. He wanted to watch Levi throw the net. Levi picked up his net, gathered the rope and net up into his right hand and with his right arm extended, he reached down and picked up and looped an edge over his index finger then reached with down with his left hand and picked up the edge closest to him and held it out to open it up some. He turned his upper body facing sideways as much as he could turn, then he gave a great level sweep of his arms as his upper body spun around and forcefully tossed it as far out over the water as far as he could and watched it open perfectly just before it landed on the surface of the water and began to sink. After a few seconds, Levi began to pull it in. He had caught a half dozen shrimp and a little fish. Blackie started seriously trying to hold them down with his paws until he could get to them.

"Good job, Levi," Michael said. Michael laughed at Blackie as he jumped on the first shrimp he saw and then the second as he was watching and strategizing about how to catch the others.

"Who is having fun now?" Levi asked Blackie and rubbed his head. "I'm ready now," said Levi.

"Do you remember how to get in?" Michael asked.

"Yeah, you have to come in from the bottom. I just hold my breath and come up underneath, right?" Levi recalled Michael telling him the last time he was here. "Yeah, that's right. I'll go first. Just follow me," Michael instructed. He went down into the water and grabbed the edge of the supership. Then, holding to the edge of the supership, he started using his hands to move around to the side to get out of the way for Levi to have room to get by. Michael showed Levi the easiest way to get in underneath without getting pulled away by the current. Levi took a deep breath, went underwater and saw the opening in the bottom. He reached up, grabbed handholds and was able to pull himself inside. Michael positioned himself right beside him and off they went, two boys on their first adventure together.

As they rounded a curve following the current through the marshlands Levi saw the dolphin on the bank. It wasn't very big. He noticed how it was unable to move and the oyster bed had cut the young dolphin in several places. It seems he had wedged himself in the middle of a rather large oyster bed and it was going to take a lot of water or a lot of muscle to get him off that jagged mess without him cutting himself up more in the process.

"How are we going to get him off of that?" Levi asked. Both boys left the supership and tried walking up the muddy embankment, slipping and sliding their way up the muddy slope avoiding the little fiddler crabs and sharp oyster shells. They made their way to the young dolphin and heard a little cry come from him.

Michael said, "I think we can pick him up. Let's try."

The two boys got as close as they could to the dolphin and precariously positioned their feet in the boggy muddy water's edge.

"You hold his head up and I'll try to get in the middle," Levi offered, "We should be able to lift him up." As the two boys got closer, the dolphin made a little squeaky sound and opened this mouth as it appeared to be looking at them. He slapped his tail once weakly.

"It's okay little fella. We're going to get you out of here," Levi said softly. So together Levi and Michael on opposite sides of the dolphin gently reached underneath the young wounded dolphin and grabbed each other's hands. As Michael hoisted up his side, Levi went down into the muck, landing on his behind on the really muddy embankment. They both started laughing. Levi got up, used his hands to wash off his pants and walked back up to the dolphin to give it another try.

"Hey, I'm ready; let's do this again, Michael." Michael thought Levi was funny but he managed to stop laughing. They got their hands under the distressed dolphin again and both stood up at the same time, lifted the dolphin up and over the remaining oyster bed, adjusted their grip and carried the young dolphin to the water.

"Okay, let's put him down here," Michael said.

The dolphin seemed to be confused and unsure if he was okay. Levi rubbed some water over his parched skin.

"He might not be able to swim too well," Levi said. Michael came close and began rubbing the little dolphin. He gave a little swish with his tail. It made a small lunge and then a second, leaving a splash of water behind and began making its way into the depths. The beautiful dolphin was going to be okay. After a few seconds Michael saw a little spout of water come up just a few feet out then head straight out toward deeper waters. "Good job," Michael said, as they looked at each other. "Good job, back," Levi returned the accolade and they slapped their hands together giving each other a big high five. "I better get back home," Levi decided he'd been gone long enough. "Okay," Michael said. They both got into the supership and headed back to Levi's house. "Want to come in for a little while if Dad's not home?" "Okay, you check, I'll wait out here." Levi got out of the supership, climbed up on the deck and ran to the house. His dad wasn't back yet so Levi ran back to the dock. "Come on!" He called to Michael, "Come in."

As they sat there playing Dungeons and Dragons on Levi's computer, Levi asked, "Do you think the dolphin is okay?"

"I think so as long as something bigger doesn't get him," Michael answered, still staring at the screen.

"Hmmm," replied Levi, "The circle of life thing." Then Levi asked rhetorically, "I wonder if he will remember us if he ever sees us again?"

Michael thought about it. "I think so," Michael concluded. "They are very smart. I bet they remember people who are nice to them."

Levi agreed. "I think so too. Maybe he'll come down this creek to visit us."

"That would be awesome," Michael said.

"So, you know about the 'circle of life' thing Michael?"

"Oh sure, I know all about that stuff. We have regular school you know, with teachers and homework," Michael explained.

"Do you go to church, too?" Levi asked.

"Yes, some of us do," Michael answered.

"You had God on your planet?" Levi asked.

"Well, not exactly the way he is here," Michael added. "Do you believe in God?" Michael asked Levi.

"Yes, I guess so," Levi answered, "Do you?" Levi asked Michael back. It only took a second for Michael to answer.

"Yeah, I mean, I like God here. My pops said when he saw the Earth for the first time; his first thought was that someone had made it. I guess he meant God."

Levi stopped there, turned his attention away from the game screen for the first time, and looked at Michael. Michael stopped and looked back at Levi. "What?" Michael finished, "He never mentioned anyone else." Michael closed his argument there as conclusive and went back to the game.

After a while longer, Michael got up to leave. Once the backdoor was slammed, Blackie came scooting around the side of the house and headed toward the dock. "Race you," Levi yelled. Both boys took off. They slowed down at the dock with Michael getting there first. "That was fun," Michael said, breathing hard. "I'll come back

Saturday if you want to do something. Check the bottle. I'll leave a note if anything changes." "Sure," Levi said as Michael slipped back into the water to board his supership. Michael stood on the dock and waved as he watched the turbulent waters calm down as the supership moved on out of the creek.

It was a cold December morning when Levi walked down to the dock and found a message in the cubbyhole spot beneath the dock. It said, "Need to see you as soon as possible. I will be back at noon." That was a couple of hours away. He must have only missed Michael by just a little while so he decided he would stay close to the dock until Michael returned. The weather was chilly but he thought Blackie might like some fresh seafood so he ran up to the garage and grabbed his shrimp net. He only had to call Blackie once and no sooner did he get it out, that he saw a little black flash come out of nowhere on to the dock, full throttle. "I think you missed me catching you some shrimp." Levi stooped down and rubbed his head, and then he adjusted his hold on the shrimp net. He gathered the rope up like a lasso and held the net up off the ground by the middle. He reached down and picked up one of the weighted edges and looped it over his index finger then used his left hand again to reach down to pick up the edge closest to him and stretch it open before a big twist with his body. He swirled around and tossed the net with enough force so that it would glide out and across the surface of the water and open up nicely there. Blackie lay in a corner, licking his paws waiting patiently for nothing in particular. He gave the rope a little tug and pulled the net in. He had a good haul this time of at least a dozen little shrimp.

"You're in luck, Blackie. Help yourself. Bon appetit," He said, and then he watched Blackie leap into action with focus and intensity to enjoy his snack. A Great White Heron walking in the marsh waters nearby caught his attention and when he turned back toward the creek entrance, he saw a whirlpool coming his way. "Here, Blackie, Michael will be happy to see you." Levi rubbed his head as Blackie was busy enjoying his unexpected feast. Once the supership got closer to the dock, it stopped where it was and the familiar white head popped up and out of the water but this time Michael was wearing an aquamarine colored suit that covered his entire body. He agilely climbed on the dock and stood beside Levi. "Wow! What are you wearing?" Levi asked?

"This is my suit so I don't get cold when it's wet," Michael said. "I brought you one too, so you can get in and out of the supership without freezing to death."

"Thanks, Michael, this is so cool," Levi said and started putting the suit on over his clothes.

"Hurry up and get it on. I need you to help me find some guys."

"Okay, where are we going?" Levi asked without hesitation.

"This is important. We have to go to Savannah, I think. That's a good place to start."

"Why?" Levi asked.

Michael began to explain, "Because I need you to help me find some people."

Levi looked at him in disbelief. "You want me to find someone?" He asked Michael, so Michael began his explanation.

"Levi, two dangerous criminals have escaped Atlantis. We need to find them. They can do incredible damage and they will too because they're mean and hate everybody. If we can spot them then we can have some of our security force capture them and bring them back. I really need your help to find them. We really don't have too many investigators out there who can look for them in the streets of Savannah. Would you please help me? I think if I can get you close and you can spot them, then we can catch them."

"Okay, but I just need to be home before dinner time or dad will start looking for me," Levi explained.

"Great! That gives us six hours," Michael exclaimed.

Levi put the soft space jump suit on and entered the supership through the opening underneath. The wetsuit made the water feel really strange against his skin. He could feel that the water was cold but it didn't make him feel cold. He felt fine. Once inside, he took the cover off of his head and waited for Michael to come in. After Michael boarded, he was excited to tell Levi the story of these two guys. He started by saying, "These two criminals are as bad as the notorious outlaws Jesse James and the Dalton Gang." Levi laughed when he heard Michael start talking about old western outlaws. "I'm not kidding," Michael said. "These are really bad guys. They shoot people and steal stuff and cause havoc and if we can't stop them then the truth about us will come out. We really need to find them before they do something else stupid and have the police chasing them too, okay?"

Levi listened and was ready to go. "How do you know they're in Savannah?" Levi asked.

Michael answered, "Because one of them had a friend there. Savannah is a big city and easy to hide out in for a while so I guess that would be a good place to start. It's not like the police in Savannah are looking for them and there aren't many of us who can help look." As soon as Levi was strapped in, Michael took off with the supership cutting beautifully through the water, hardly leaving a wake.

Coming up the mouth of the Savannah River, Michael avoided all the other boat traffic, some boats were adorned with Christmas decorations and silver garland sparkling in the sunlight and others with brightly colored Christmas decorations. He struggled in dealing with the strong turbulent current to hold his supership steady. The waters were very dark and visibility was mere feet. He finally came up to the surface so they could look out the panoramic window.

When they got close to River Street, Michael veered out of the main current and began slowly cruising the river adjacent to the street. Even during the day they could see all the Christmas lights and colors lighting up the trees along the street as they cruised up the Savannah river. He loved looking at the reflections of the red, green and blue sparkling lights among the festive decorations in the stores along River Street. Seasonal floral arrangements with lots of red ribbons on evergreen wreaths and Santa displays adorned the stores and restaurant windows everywhere. People were walking along the sidewalk wearing heavy coats and locking arms to stay warm while listening to the Christmas music that filled the air. He even saw a street vendor dressed as Santa, playing his guitar on the corner for change. He saw the skyline of Savannah and the Talmadge Bridge as they approached the world famous red brick street boardwalk at the water's edge.

Levi got out of the sub without being seen. He climbed up onto the boardwalk and took off the waterproof spacesuit, looked right and left and decided he would go left. On the ride over Michael had him study the men's pictures and what they might be wearing. Levi thought he might start looking in all the restaurants along the water's edge. He went into Snoopy's and didn't see anyone who looked like them there and then next door to the Cookie Factory and the Fudge Factory where he had enough money to buy some chocolate. He peeked into the flag store where all the bright red, green and yellows of the beautiful colorful flags and kites hung from the ceiling. He went into another small restaurant and lo and behold even a little rhyme came into his mind. "…and what to his wandering eyes did appear but the unmistakable look of two aliens drinking beer."

He turned around and walked out of the restaurant before he was seen and ran all the way back to the supership. He didn't see the supership at first as he walked slowly looking down close to the water's edge and all of a sudden there came a little white head below the street level so no one could see him. "Hey, up there," Michael called. "Hey, I found them!" Levi exclaimed. "They are right down there," he pointed, "in that restaurant!"

"Okay! We have to hurry!" Michael ducked back out of sight. Levi waited on the boardwalk with his eyes fixed on the restaurant door where the two men were right now. Michael called the security force that was already close by and told them to head toward the restaurant where the two men were spotted. Michael came back to the surface. Levi pulled the chocolate out of his pocket and handed

Michael some. His eyes lit up. "Thanks," he said as he popped it into his mouth. "Michael, they're still in that restaurant down the street. Somebody needs to get over there right now. I can show the security guys where they are if they hurry."

"Already on it," Michael responded like a policeman. I radioed our security force and told them where they were. I gave them this location and told him that we had spotted them on River Street and to hurry," Michael concluded.

"I better go see where they go in case they leave the restaurant," Levi said.

"That's a great idea," Michael said. "I'll stay right here and watch you and let you know when security gets here."

"Okay," Levi said, and then he got up and ran back towards the restaurant as fast as he could. Just as he jerked open the door, he ran straight into one of the men coming out. Levi stopped, looked up and froze. The two extremely pale men gave him a stern look and walked on past him. Levi stopped, turned around and sat on the bench outside the restaurant so he could watch them go down the street. He decided he was going to have to follow them as they continued down the sidewalk until security could get here. He knew they would be gone from sight soon. It was after one o'clock in the afternoon. He had time so he guessed it'd be alright if he followed them a little ways. He was at least twenty steps behind the two when he got up off his chair. Several people were in between him and them by then so it was easy for him to keep his distance but he was careful not to take his eyes off them for a second. When they came up on the street they crossed into this Bank of America branch office. He didn't know if he should leave to find someone or not. He looked around for someone he thought might look like an alien in a security cop uniform. He didn't see anyone then he remembered what Michael said about these two being like Jesse James and robbing banks, what if they're going to rob this bank? He didn't want to leave to find someone and run back just in case maybe they weren't going to rob it. He crossed the street and went up to the front door of the bank. He couldn't see anything but his own reflection in the tinted glass.

He was feeling a bit anxious but he went inside anyway. He immediately saw the two men looking around. As one of them was reaching toward his waistline for what Levi thought might be a gun, he spotted a fire alarm on the wall. He walked straight up to it and with several patrons watching, he pulled it down and just as it began to go off he ran out the door across the street and saw Michael's familiar white face under a hat. "Let's get out of here!" Levi exclaimed. "I'm in trouble for sure!"

"Wait!" yelled Michael. Levi stopped, "Look!" Michael pointed to two men in regular clothes and heavy coats coming their way. "Hey over here, he motioned them over." The two men looked his way. "Quick, come here." The two men ran to Levi.

"Michael! What are you doing here?" The officer seemed a little upset.

"Shut up Mark." Michael snapped back.

"We're doing your job for you. We found the guys you're looking for, is what," Michael said back in a snarky way. "Those guys you are looking for were about to rob that bank is all, so Levi pulled the fire alarm to stop them."

"There they go now!" Levi pointed to the two men who just exited the bank and were headed down the street.

"Okay, let's go," One officer said to the other one. The security agents took off after them leaving Levi and Michael. Both boys stood transfixed; looking in the direction the officers went to catch the criminals until they couldn't see anyone or hear anything anymore. The fire alarm went silent.

"Wow! That was great, Levi," Michael said. "You were perfect. You are the perfect agent."

"You knew that guy, Mark?" Levi asked, almost impressed.

"Yeah, he went to school with my brother. He'd hang out at home sometimes. He can be a jerk, too."

"Oh," Levi said, "How do we know if they caught the guys?"

"Don't worry. They will be back in jail by tonight. They just needed to find them quickly. I think we're all done here, Watson," Michael stated with a terrible English accent.

They both were still laughing as Levi slipped back into the water and hurriedly got back into the supership. Michael wanted to recant every detail of how it all went down and asked Levi, "You could see them standing inside the bank about to rob it?" Michael asked.

"Yeah," Levi said. "I didn't know what to do so I just pulled the fire alarm." "Ha ha ha!" They both laughed out loud.

"That was great thinking." "Just think if you could have been in an old western bank while it was being robbed by Jesse James. Imagine you were right there, just like that! What would you have done then?" Michael asked.

"I don't know," Levi answered, "do you think they might have had a fire alarm?" They both started laughing. Levi looked at the time. "I better get back home. Let's play D&D," he suggested.

"Okay," Michael accepted the invitation as Levi put on his jumpsuit. They swam back to the supership, got in and headed to Levi's.

CHAPTER SEVENTEEN

At school, Levi was looking forward to Christmas break. He had left a message for Michael at the dock that the Christmas Boat Parade was going down the Ogeechee River Saturday night. He told Michael to come about five o'clock if he wanted to go. It would be fun to watch it from the supership. Michael got the message and couldn't wait to go.

He showed up Saturday on time and they quickly headed to watch the Ogeechee River Christmas Boat Parade. They found a good place to stop and observe the parade from the supership. They were ready when the first of the boats started up the river. They heard the music the moment they surfaced. "Here Comes Santa Claus" was blasting across the water. Smaller decorated boats were close by watching the parade as well. The first in line was a sailboat with colored blinking lights strung down from the masthead to the deck with a fully decorated tree on the bow. Beside the tree sat ladies in heavy coats in front of a fake fire. The next was a fishing trawler lit up from top to deck with hanging lights and a big Merry Christmas sign. The crew was dressed as elves and Mrs. Clause was handing out cookies. The line of boats got longer. Michael pointed at one that looked like it had a spaceship crash on it and Santa was there handing out presents. There must have been more than twenty boats this year.

There was one boat decorated like the middle of Whoville, with the crew standing around the town's Christmas tree singing, "Fah who Foraze, Dah who Doraze, Welcome Christmas, Christmas

Day." Levi pointed at the decorated palm trees on another sailboat and the horns started blasting and music started blaring from the marina. Loud voices echoing across the water was a sure sign that the marina was where everyone was meeting up after the parade.

Levi finally sat back in his seat. Michael was still looking out. "That was great, wasn't it?" Levi asked.

"Yeah," Michael agreed.

Levi then said, "Let's go back to my house. Dad has a late date tonight."

"Okay," Michael accepted.

They made it back and both went inside. The house had a decorated tree now with a few festively wrapped presents underneath and a nativity scene set up with models on the coffee table. "I like your tree," Michael said. "It's okay," Levi turned the lights on and it came to life. Some lights twinkled while others stayed on. "Want something to drink?" Levi asked. "Sure," Michael said. Levi brought back a couple of blue Ocean Splash Energy drinks. They both opened their bottles at the same time. They positioned their bottles against their lips. "Ready, set, Go!" Levi said and the two boys began chugging the drinks. Levi hit the table with his empty bottle first. Michael put his down with still a couple of swallows left. "Wow! You must have been dying of thirst," Michael said.

"I was," Levi agreed.

They sat down and opened up D&D and resumed their game. "Did you have anything like boats and stuff on your planet?" Levi asked.

"Yes, but everything was different there. I don't really know except what I saw in some graphic artist pictures," Michael explained, "I remember the story my mom used to tell me when I was little about the day we got here, July 7th, 1947. We had been traveling toward Earth for centuries. Betelgeuse is 650 light years from Earth and that's the solar system where Tyrol was. Light travels at 186,000 miles per hour. So it would take you 650 years if you could travel at 186,000 miles an hour. You do the math," he paused. "Anyway, we couldn't stay there because Betelgeuse is a dying star. It turned into a red giant and began expanding and we knew that one day it would totally engulf Tyrol. Anyway, mom said they could see the Earth getting bigger and bluer as they got closer and then the atmosphere with clouds, but then they realized it was heavily populated with an advanced civilization. They started picking up signals from Earth. The captain knew this was it for them. Do or die. They couldn't risk being turned away and once they hit the atmosphere, things got hot, over 3000 degrees. It melted some stuff and there was no turning back. Once through the atmosphere we were here to stay."

"That must have been scary, losing control and crashing," Levi said.

"Yeah," Michael explained, "A couple of superships, bigger than mine, were able to get out of our ship on entry. One was so damaged that it wound up crashing in Roswell, New Mexico." Levi looked at Michael transfixed by what he was hearing. "Yep," Michael said. "That was one of ours. We never got it back, but the main ship was coming in hot right into the ocean where it still is today. Everyone thought we would get searched down and killed but what happened was incredible. The army started covering it up for us with some dumb story about weather balloons and something called a Mogul world radiation monitor or something like that. Anyway, that wasn't what it was. The truth is under your nose!" Michael said in a deep voice to imitate the opening sequence line from, The X Files.

Levi couldn't think of a thing to say to all that, except to ask, "Did anyone survive?"

"We are pretty sure a couple of them did survive but we never were able to confirm that." Michael answered as best he could.

Then Levi asked, "Is this supership the same kind of spaceship that crashed?"

"Sort of," Michael said. "This one is a much newer model."

They played a little longer until it was about time for his dad to get home, and then walked out to the dock. Blackie came rushing past on his way to the end of the dock. "Blackie, I don't have my net!" Levi called to his cat. Blackie didn't seem to notice.

"When are you coming back?" Levi asked.

"I don't know, maybe Saturday if you aren't doing anything," Michael answered.

"Okay, sounds good. I'll leave you a message in a few days," Michael said.

"Okay, see ya!" Levi said waving bye as Michael went underwater and out of sight to get into his supership. Levi turned and headed up to the house, grabbed his net and came back to catch a snack for Blackie.

Michael left the river and hit the strong currents of the open ocean and pushed the home button on the dashboard. As he was racing through the water, he saw something on his radar. It was huge. He headed toward the surface and came to a halt. He looked through his panoramic window but could see nothing. It was right up on him. "A sub!" he said under his breath. He let his ship drift down deeper as the sub moved fast past him. He could see an insignia on the side. "Russian!" Michael said out loud. He hesitated, deciding what to do. He followed it for about ten minutes. "What are you going to do?" he asked himself. "Any good 007 secret agent would never let a Russian sub pass unchecked into these American waters."

Without further hesitation he said out loud as he sat alone in his faithful supership, "Don't worry America, I got this." He locked his radar on the sub and set a course to follow America's enemy. He wanted to know what they were up to.

Levi sat in his room thinking about Michael. He wanted his dad to meet him. How should he introduce him, as a friend or school mate? He thought the best story could be something like, this is my friend Michael. He has a medical condition and is home schooled." He paused again. "That won't work either." Dad will want to meet his parents. "Hey, Mr. Benjamin, we're Michael's parents, you know, the aliens who live in a spaceship sitting on the bottom of the ocean. It's nice to meet you." Levi decided to wait to introduce Michael.

On Saturday, Levi wrote a note and put it in the bottle. He was surprised there wasn't a note from Michael already in there. Michael had not been there at all this week. The next day he walked to the dock and saw his note had not been touched. Levi wanted to see Michael again before Christmas. He had bought a little St. Christopher charm and chain for him to wear around his neck for protection and wanted to give it to him. He even wrapped it in a little box with wrapping paper and a bright red bow. Michael didn't come by. Days passed, December first came and went and Levi still didn't know what had happened to Michael but he was starting to think it wasn't good. For the first time in a while, he thought about Abby Mortensen.

CHAPTER EIGHTEEN

Capt. Collevechio and his crew continued their service for the US Coast Guard. They were diligent in their work and knew the importance of their cause. They were well aware of stories of how the Bermuda Triangle held mysteries still unexplained and of others that have run across unidentified submerged objects, USOs, which were still a mystery. They kept their eyes open and Capt. Collevechio was determined that if he ever caught any of them on radar again, he would pursue them to their source. He didn't report his encounter to his commanding officer. None of his crew ever wrote anything down that would create more questions than answers, so the Bermuda Triangle still held mysteries in her deep waters. The crew would talk about it to each other and to other sailors they would meet. Sea stories and legends would continue to grow and be passed along.

In Baltimore, there lived a mother and daughter who knew the truth. In Savannah, a young boy had a close encounter of his own. It was an unlikely encounter where two young boys from different worlds became friends and would play together and travel great distances underwater together. There was an innocence of youth present that was not spoiled by skepticism and fear of the unknown. Their friendship started with the mutual trust of children, by talking for hours, by exploring and investigating things together and relying on each other to act as a partner or teammate, to eventually becoming friends for life. There was innocence where things unique to each of them were shared with honesty and trust. This was a different kind of contact. You couldn't put a number on it. There were already stories of contact between humans and aliens of the first, second and third kinds, all fiction. This was different. This was real. This was what Levi would later label as, "Friendship: Contact of the Best Kind," so it was no surprise that Levi wanted to know what happened to his friend Michael.

PART TWO

CHAPTER NINETEEN

Friendship: Contact of the Best Kind

Michael was submersed in his supership and on his way home from Levi's dock when out of nowhere a Russian submarine nearly collided with him. The next thing he knew, he was following it. He tried to stay hidden from the sub's radar by staying in the turbulence and stirred up sediment created by its propellers but he was picked up on the sub's sophisticated radar right away. Most of the turbulence dissipated quickly in the saturated waters and it was impossible to remain hidden.

The tropical ocean waters still captured light from the day's sunlight and its blue hues ranged from deep Baltic blues to lighter pastel shades that blended seamlessly with the horizon's sky. Michael felt exposed in the quickly clearing waters but thought it was important for the Russians to know that THEY had been spotted, too. Suddenly the Russian sub came to an, "All Stop." He saw the sub launch a small drone sub equipped with cameras so he figured it was time to go. Michael didn't feel like getting his picture taken today so he pulled up abruptly on his controls without looking to his left. He made the extreme bank, not realizing an old wreck that had been lying there for over a century had a mast head sticking right out in his path. He jerked sharply on the control and in doing so jammed a stabilizer necessary for maneuvering underwater. Suddenly, no matter what Michael did he couldn't unstick the controls and he was headed down. He had no way to maneuver to the surface and was going deeper. "Uh oh," Michael said under his breath. "I'm going to miss you old buddy," he said to his supership as he prepared to abandon her. The drone along with the Russian sub disappeared out of sight as Michael escaped his damaged supership.

He had no trouble swimming to the surface, he had done this before. He would take a half breath to reduce pressure and just slowly swim and allow the air in his lungs to carry him up. He guessed it wouldn't take more than fifteen to twenty seconds to do that so he was certain that he would be fine. "No problem," he said under his breath. He didn't like Russians snooping around and had no regrets about losing his supership. He's seen 007 abandon his top-end and loaded Aston Martins, without even blinking, plenty of times. He came to the surface, took a deep breath, looked around and saw an island far off. He started swimming in that direction.

Darkness closed in around Michael while he was still miles from the island and he began to hear something. He heard water occasionally, moving forcefully, above the slight splashing noises he was making swimming along. It sounded rhythmic to him, manmade. Suddenly he was startled when his leg brushed up against some floating seaweed. It felt like he had dozed off and suddenly awakened. His mind reacted quickly and his imagination got the best of him. His first thought was of sharks. He swirled around looking in all directions for a fin but couldn't see very far from his perspective low in the water. He felt like his heart was going to pound out of his chest. The cool salty water was continuously sloshing into his face and eyes and getting into his mouth and ears with each stroke and his arms were getting fatigued. Gusting winds made it difficult to hear much but he heard this rhythmic noise again. It sounded like a large boat with many paddles being quietly paddled by him in the darkness. He stopped swimming and listened, even looked around but he couldn't see any lights from a boat out here with him. He was in the pitch black darkness now. The sound of rushing water was steady and the swirling sound didn't stop. He was sure he could hear it plain as day. It sounded like long paddles would sound, pulling a large ship along. He had in his mind a picture of a Viking ship with oars. He definitely heard water being pulled and splashed by paddles with an occasional bump of wood on wood echoing across the mostly choppy waters. It sounded like a big boat to Michael. It made the sound an old ship with sails would make and it sounded like it was getting louder, like it was moving closer now. A slight wind carried sounds of sailing sheets rustling in the darkness. Suddenly, the light of the moon reflected just for a second off what Michael was sure was, the head-on bow of a large, wooden ship with dingy white sails. It came into view when the moon found a clearing between swiftly moving clouds and then was hidden again behind the next dark and heavy cloud set.

He got only one quick glimpse of the ship before it went completely back into the darkness. Michael gasped, he couldn't believe his eyes. He saw it for one brief moment. It looked ghostly and hidden in the darkness but it was coming right towards him. He heard no human sounds or any sounds of life coming from it at all. Then all the blood left his legs and he just treaded water looking all around. The ship was coming toward him and he became frightened. He didn't know what to do. He couldn't get spotted or they might try to rescue him. He tried to stay low in the water and stayed quiet. As it approached him, he could only hear it. He tried to make himself invisible by going underwater and counting to ten but he was afraid he would be hit by the boat or the oars. He tried to stay longer but that was all the breath he had left. He decided he would go back up, take a quick breath and go back down deeper, but when he came up the ship was gone. Michael could neither see nor hear the ship anymore. In ten seconds the ghostly ship was gone. Darkness had wrapped it up and the sea had carried it away.

As hours passed the temperature started dropping and Michael felt a chill. He was nearing the island and could clearly see lights across the shoreline now, including many Christmas lights on trees and bushes. It wasn't a good thing for him that it was inhabited but he had no choice. Once there he hoped to figure out how to get home without being discovered. In the meantime, he was going to need a place to hide. As he got closer to the island he noticed it was very quiet. He heard a car horn and then a few dogs began barking. He saw a fishing dock lit up with floodlights so he turned towards the dock. He saw a shrimp boat and several smaller fishing boats but didn't see anyone around the dock so he climbed up onto the dock and stayed low as he looked around until he finally found a place to sit down out of direct sight of any open areas behind a boatshed. He was wearing his waterproof suit he wore for getting in and out of the supership when the water was cool. He was dry but he still felt a chill so he hunkered down in a corner. He had just closed his eyes and was drifting off when a voice startled him awake.

"Where did you come from, little mate?" the words came from a rough looking fisherman reeking of whiskey.

"Nowhere, leave me alone!" Michael stated back sternly.

"Oh, okay little mate. I thought you might need some help. I saw you swimming toward the dock from a good distance out. I figured you didn't swim out there, that's why I wasn't sure what you were at first. When I saw your head, I thought you were a manatee," the fisherman finished. Michael thought that was funny, he grinned but didn't laugh and he wasn't ready to say anything. The old guy had caught him off guard. He hadn't expected to get spotted so fast and he didn't have a story yet.

"When's the last time you had something to eat?" the fisherman continued.

"I don't know," Michael said. He hadn't eaten since early that morning and he was hungry.

The fisherman said, "Follow me," and got up and headed back to his shrimp boat. Once inside the captain threw some bacon in a frying pan and got out the eggs. "How do you like your eggs?" the captain asked.

"Scrambled is fine," Michael answered.

The captain poured himself a cup of coffee, leaving room for a large shot of Jack Daniels as he stood at his skillet frying up everything. "I never saw you around here before," the captain said. "Where'd you come from?" he asked.

"Nowhere," Michael said.

"Well, where's your parents?" he asked next. Michael didn't say anything. "Okay, then," the captain said as he sat a plate of bacon and scrambled eggs in front of him. "What's your name?"

"Michael," he said.

"Okay Michael, people call me, Cap. Well, are you lost or a runaway or something?" the captain asked. "Do you need to call your parents?"

Michael didn't know what to say right then so he settled with, "You have a phone?"

"No, I don't have much need for a phone the way I move around. No signal out here anyway. You'd have to go to one of the bigger islands around here to pick up a signal," Cap informed him.

"How far is the closest one?" he asked the fisherman.

"Oh, I'd say about an eight hour trip with this old tub but I'm not headed in that direction. Tomorrow you can go talk to the local constable and they might be able to help you."

Disappointed, Michael just looked down and said, "I'm fine."

"Okay, well, you can bunk down over there if you want. I get up pretty early so if you don't want to become part of the crew, you'd better be off this boat before it leaves the dock or else you might be swimming back here again tomorrow." Michael couldn't hold back a smile that time.

"Yes Sir, Cap," Michael answered back. Then, the captain turned on the radio. A local station came on playing reggae music. Michael liked hearing the steel drum beat and the voice of some Marley singing, as he relaxed for the first time and went to sleep.

It was just before dawn when Michael was woken by heavy footsteps on the deck. The entire boat seemed to creak and vibrate with each heavy step and he could hear things being moved around too. He heard nets being dragged as old boards were creaking under each sure-footed step. Cap was checking his nets and lines before leaving the dock like he always did, knowing it was easier to do work here on the calm waters at the dock than to have to make any repairs while riding constant waves. The entire boat just rocked too much when it wasn't tied. The only other noise was the light but steady slapping sound of small waves splashing against the boat's hull. Michael loved those sounds and thought it would be fun to be a shrimp boat captain. He got up and stuck his head out the hatch to see what was happening. A flock of squawking seabirds caught his attention as a group of five pelicans soared effortlessly past in perfect formation following the water's shoreline and holding steady in the strong ocean breeze. The sun was about to come up and was starting to change the colors of the sky on the Eastern horizon now. Clouds there were turning beautiful shades of orange-red to magenta and purple. He heard a noise and looked around at Cap. He was tying a line and folding his last net, preparing to head out. He had a good day yesterday and had used his earnings to refill the gas tanks and cupboard with the required Jack Daniels and coffee. He was wearing a beat up old captain's hat and carrying his coffee cup. He was about ready to leave and he looked up at the odd looking boy in front of him now. He had seen a lot of odd looking kids around before but he could swear this little guy looked different than anyone he had ever seen. There was something odd about the shape of his head but he had seen a lot of odd looking people in his lifetime so he let it go. It was obvious that he was from around here somewhere so he didn't push him for answers.

Michael climbed on up the ladder to the deck and saw Cap walking around his net and rigging.

"How're you feeling?" Cap asked.

"I'm fine," Michael answered.

"So, then, are you going over to the police department? See if they can get you in touch with some of your people? That might not be a bad idea, you know? Get you back home," Cap finished.

"No, you said something about how maybe I could become part of the crew?" Michael asked.

Cap looked up at him and said, "No, I said if you weren't off the boat by the time I pulled away from the dock, you might become part of the crew. I was just joking, Michael. How old are you?"

"Eleven going on twelve," Michael answered.

"I don't know, Michael. Where are your parents?"

Michael thought for a second and said, "I want to go home too, Cap but I have to be careful who I talk to. It's Top Secret stuff."

"Oh, I see," Cap nodded. "You don't want to talk to the police, right?"

"That's right, Cap. I do want to go home. I just have to figure out how to get there."

"I was looking at you and you just don't look healthy to me. I mean, you're so pale," Cap expressed concern.

Then, just as Michael was about to tell him a made up story, that's when Cap unexpectedly asked, "Do you have leukemia or liver disease or something?"

"No, Cap," Michael answered.

"You didn't run away to die did you? You got some sort of bucket list?" he asked Michael.

"Ha, ha," Michael laughed. He hadn't expected to hear that and burst out. "No, Cap! I'm perfectly healthy," Michael said, grinning back.

Then Cap sat down and put on his old ragged Captain's thinking cap. He took a sip of his cool coffee and said, "I had a first mate up until his wife went into labor yesterday. If you need a job to earn a few bucks and don't get seasick, I could use a second pair of hands on this trip."

"Okay," Michael answered, "I do!" and eagerly accepted the offer.

"Do you know anything about shrimp boat fishing?"

"No Cap," Michael eagerly stated, "...but I don't get seasick," Michael answered back.

"Yeah, well, that's good," Cap responded. He then looked hard at the kid and said, "Ok, you're going to have to listen to me when I tell you something."

"Yes sir, Cap," Michael replied like he was in the Navy.

"Just do what I tell you. It'll be alright," Cap concluded.

"Yes Sir, Cap," Michael answered back. Cap looked back to see if he read any sarcasm in this boy's overly enthusiastic answer and odd looking eyes but he didn't.

"Ok, get up here and I'll show you how this works." Michael jumped up and that's when the captain suggested he put something else on. He told Michael there were coveralls and an old cap below that he could wear. Michael hurried down, put them on and hurried back.

Cap kept working as he talked, "I got a few rules then. Number one is, once we pull away from the dock there is no turning back and we will be out until I say it is time to come back. Number two, as a crew member you're expected to carry out all orders without delay and to do so to the best of your ability."

"Yes Sir, Cap," Michael said.

"A simple, Aye, will do," he replied.

"Aye, Cap!" Michael exclaimed anxiously with a growing grin on his face.

"Help yourself to the coffee. I'm guessing you can make your own breakfast," and went back to his work.

When Michael finished his breakfast and washed his plate, he climbed the ladder back up to the deck where he saw Cap checking everything again that he checked yesterday and this morning. Now he was at the engine checking the old engine's oil level and not forgetting to check that the batteries were fully charged.

When Cap looked up and saw Michael standing there, he said, "Come on over here." He turned his attention towards the nets and lines. Cap reached down and picked up a portion of rope that will be used to haul the nets out of the water. "Do you know how to tie a half-hitch?" His voice was getting louder over the noises all around.

"No, Cap" Michael answered and hurried over to watch Cap tie one.

"Ok, pay attention. A half-hitch is a very strong knot to haul heavy nets out of the water but there is another reason to use it. When they are done right, and we pull the nets onto the boat and they are ready to untie, a quick tug on the other side and the entire catch is dumped at once and can cover the deck. Aye!" he shook his head. "It's a beautiful sight because it means all your hard work has been worth it. The half-hitch is strong but easy to untie, so that's the first knot you'll learn today." The experienced fisherman deftly looped the line smoothly and perfectly in a series of three separate loops and cinches over top of each other. The big knot forming mesmerized Michael and made him want to try. He caught on quickly with the one-on-one lesson, then Cap got up and asked, "Do you see those two long outriggers there?" He pointed to two tall steel poles that right now were pointing straight up. "Once we leave the dock here, I'm going to lower them a bit to help steady the boat. It's for the same reason a tightrope walker uses a long pole to stabilize his balance on a tightrope. Leaving those heavy poles in the upright position with all that weight so high and pointed straight up could cause the boat to be unstable and list or even capsize in heavy seas, so shrimp boats travel this way over choppy waters as soon as they get away from the dock. They make my girl steady on rough seas," he reflected before going on.

"We have four nets, two for each outrigger. I lower those outriggers down on both sides and we run two nets out on each one by lines that are attached to these doors here to the end of the outrigger, making sure nothing's tangled and the weighted sides of the nets are down, that's the side that glides across the bottom, you see? This piece of chain is a part of the net as well. It goes in front of the bottom of the net and is pulled across the ocean bed ahead of the net. It's called a tickler. Its purpose is to scare shrimp up off the bottom. The top side has floats to hold up the top of the nets and it will hold them all open at the same time, you see?" Michael nodded.

Cap got up, walked around to the pilot house and started the big engine of his boat to listen to it run. He could tell if something wasn't right just by listening to it now. He kept talking as Michael followed close behind him, Cap's voice was booming over the loud noise of the engine.

He got up and walked back out onto the deck to continue Michael's lesson. Cap pointed to the two wooden doors lying beside the net. "These are the two doors I mentioned before. He picked one up and showed Michael how one side of the door was attached to the netting and the other side was attached to the lines and pulley system. Each door is gently lowered over the side by hand and pulled out to the end of the outrigger, along with the nets attached to it, by pulley lines. The boat is set at a slow speed as the nets are slowly positioned in the water and held in place by the weight of the moving current. The doors with the nets attached go all the way to the bottom, which is where the shrimp are. The doors stay in position at the front of each side of the net and rely totally on the force of the current to separate and hold the net wide open as it glides across the ocean bed." He pointed to the various parts of this operation and how it all worked as he talked. "We pull it along behind the boat, scaring up shrimp with this front part here that drags on the bottom and scoops them up into these bags here that will be tied to the back of the nets using this knot you just learned to tie. That's how we secure the bag at the very end of this net that funnels everything back to the bag. It's got a couple of escape hatches built in for sea turtles and fish, but it's as simple as that. You think you can handle it?" Cap finished.

"Yeah, Cap. Just tell me what to do," Michael stated eagerly.

"Ok, just have a seat. We got a ways to go," Cap said.

Cap walked around to the pilot's seat and took his seat, put both hands on the wheel, looked at Michael and said, "Let's go find some shrimp!" Cap didn't smile but Michael did. "Now position yourself up here so you can see what I'm doing and watch where we're going, in case I fall off the boat you can come get me. Otherwise I might find MYSELF swimming home tonight." Michael knew he was kidding around reminding him about watching him swim up to the dock last night. "I can teach you about signs."

"Signs?" Michael asked.

"Yep," Cap continued as he revved up the shrimp boat's motor, scaring pelicans off all the pylons as they pulled away from the dock. "I like to look for birds," Cap said. "Birds are a good sign that a big school of something is under them, so we may be able to pull in a good haul of fish too. Sometimes my old instincts are spot on, but that's old school. I still have my depth gauges and I've fished here many years. I've got a good idea where to start. The thing about shrimp is they are an annual crop. They replenish their population every year like a crop of corn except you don't have to plant shrimp." Michael thought that sounded funny. "They have their corn harvester and I have my shrimp harvester. I catch a lot of conch too. They tear up my net but folks love fritters and they buy a lot of those big ole conch shells, too."

Michael sat next to Cap, who would occasionally mumble something under his breath that Michael could only half-hear through all the noise. The wind blowing into his ears made it hard to hear too but he didn't mind and inhaled a deep breath through his nose as he looked ahead. He smelled the salty spray in his face. It was a familiar smell he always could pick out. It was the awesome smell of the great Atlantic Ocean. He was excited and ready to get started. He hadn't given much thought about how to get home. Right now he was looking at the ocean, the waves and the occasional dolphin pods that swam along with them.

As the boat approached an area Cap had fished many times, he cut the speed of the boat to idle and the boat began to slow down. Cap got up and walked to the nets, continuing to talk. "The main purpose of having the outriggers is for fishing like I told you. They hold the nets out away from the boat and keep each side of the net open and far from the other side when pulling them along behind the boat. That's shrimping."

"I got it Cap," Michael repeated. "Each side of the boat, the port and starboard, has its own outrigger and each outrigger holds two cone-shaped but separate nets side by side on the bottom and it's important they don't become tangled as we lower them into the water. So, the boat has four nets total with two on each side," he repeated.

"That's right and over there the nets are already fitted with blocks, floats and cables and the leg lines are all connected. You don't have to fool with any of that unless you see a problem. Then let me know." Cap pointed to a place on the deck.

"Now, I'll tell you about the nets. You see them lying there all neatly folded?" Cap pointed to a big pile on the deck. "We're going to unfold them. Pay attention when you unfold them because they have to be folded back that way when we're done,"

"Yes sir, Cap," Michael yelled over the motors and noises around him. His eyes were fixed now on the pile of netting.

"Now picture this in your mind so you will know how it's supposed to look. It helps you recognize when something's not right." Michael turned his way a moment so he could hear well. "The doors are standing up like doors down there on each side of the nets on the bottom. The floating portion of the netting would be attached to the top of the door and the other end of the board, the bottom, is attached to the weighted portion of the netting. So if these simple doors are hooked up right and dropped over the side, they not only separate the top from bottom but also keeps it from closing in on the sides. They would look like two open doors at each side of the net like the open doors of a big old church. If you swam in front of it...like a fish, it would scoop you up," he stopped there and Michael looked up at him. "Got it?" Cap yelled over the noise. Michael shook his head vigorously. "Yeah, you got it. You're a smart lad. Just because you got it doesn't mean you can do it," Cap paused, looked hard at Michael and continued back with the lesson. "Once the net is lying on the bottom, it resembles a flat-sided ice cream cone. The part that lays on the bottom, the bottom line, has weights to hold it down, while the top line has floats to hold that part up," Michael was getting it.

"Do you remember how to tie that half hitch?" Cap yelled.

"Yes, Cap." Then the captain pointed to the line and where to tie the bag onto the net. He continued to hold the boat steady and oversee Michael's work. Cap asked Michael to hold up the knot he tied so he could check it and then he gave it a good tug to tighten it. Michael watched and realized quickly that he needed to pull his knots tighter. He would hate it if the knot came loose while holding a net full of shrimp. He would remember to give it that extra tug from now on.

Once that was done, and without commenting on Michael's knots, Cap turned and asked him, "Are you ready, Michael?" Michael shook his head that he was ready. "Ok, I'm going to do this first one then you do the next. He put his motor in gear. And lifted the first door over the port side and used electric motors attached to the pulley system to pull the door and nets out to the end of the outrigger, then began to lower it into the water. Michael watched it as the netting was fed over the side. Michael could feel the vibration and drag on the boat as the netting weighed heavily on the engines. "Let's go starboard. You do this one and I'll watch."

Michael tied another bag onto a net, gave it an extra tug, and looked up at Cap for his approval. Cap gave it an approving nod and Michael then tied the second bag on the other net and gave it an extra tug too. He walked over and strained to pick up the heavy door, looked to make sure everything was free from any obstruction, and eased it over the side. Cap ran the door out on the outrigger and began lowering it into the water. Everything was going smoothly.

After a few minutes, when Cap was satisfied the strain on his old faithful boat became enough, he started the motors to bring up the nets and haul in the catch. "Okay, Michael. Grab the first bag and swing it over the deck!" Cap ordered as he operated the controls. Michael looked at Cap for approval to go ahead and open the full, heavy bag. When Cap gave the go ahead, Michael gave a few hard tugs on the wet slip knot and finally it slipped open at Michael's feet and at least fifty pounds of shrimp and fish, conch and starfish, oyster shells and various medium and small fish covered his feet.

"WOW!" Michael yelled.

"Okay, Michael! Watch out for that little shark over there and that stingray too. Throw everything back except the shrimp, conch and fish over about a foot long! Move along! As fast as you can! We're going to make another run as soon as we get this catch below!" Michael worked as fast as he could so it only took a minute to go through the entire catch. "Open that hatch there!" He pointed to his storage compartment. "Push them in there! Hurry along!" Michael was working like a pit-stop crew chief changing a tire at the Daytona 500. He was sure he couldn't hurry any faster. Cap watched but kept quiet.

The enthusiastic first mate worked hard and fast and began to pull up the netting to get to the end. He knew he would have to tie the bag back on so he got started. Cap let him go and began getting the rigging ready for another pass. Once the rigging was set, he walked back to check Michael's work. He had good knots on the bags so he picked one up and started throwing it overboard while Michael helped. They made another pass with equally good results. After the third pass, the fish well had close to two hundred pounds of fish and shrimp in it and the gas was getting low so Cap decided they would head back to the dock although Michael had readied the netting for another pass if Cap wanted to.

Like an experienced deckhand, Michael leaped off the boat at the fisherman's co-op dock and swung the load onto the dock. No one paid any attention to Michael except to help him with the catch. He was still wearing the ball cap and coveralls Cap had given him earlier. Cap got the weight of his catch and accepted another good day's pay for their hard work. It was a short ride to the gas pumps and a check of oil levels and net condition and then they headed back to the dock where they started out that morning.

On the way back to the dock, Michael looked up at the old man he liked a lot. "Cap?" he asked.

"Yes, Michael," Cap looked at Michael seriously.

"Cap, how did you become a shrimp boat Captain?"

"Hmmm, well I guess you'd have to say I was raised doing it. When I was little I lived in Charleston. I didn't get to go to college. I liked fishing though, did all kinds of it as a kid, shrimping, crabbing, fishing until one day I was at Captain Jack's Seafood Restaurant near the beach and who do you think was working there that day? Capt. Jack himself. We started talking and I asked him if his seafood was caught around here. He said he caught most of it himself, that he had a boat and everything. I said I'd like to go out on one someday. Well, he invited me out the next morning. So, there I was on a shrimp boat that fast. I've been doing it pretty much ever since."

They pulled up to the dock where they had been that morning and Michael hustled onto the dock to tie off the lines to the moorings. Cap began his routine he had every day to begin inspecting his operation from front to back. Michael watched and helped where he could. He wanted to learn how to be a shrimp boat captain.

It was almost dark and Michael felt sleepy after eating a belly full of boiled shrimp cooked up by Cap. He had boiled a couple of pounds of shrimp in Louisiana Shrimp boil and cut up two big Idaho potatoes and put it all in a pot, then added Old Bay seasoning with a double dusting of red pepper powder and topped it off with a couple of good sprinkles of crushed red pepper. Michael's mouth began watering just before things started heating up. He drank a big cup of water although he didn't think it helped much. As hot as it was, he thought it was the greatest meal he ever tasted. Once he finished, he sat down and got so sleepy that he decided to lie down on his cot. Cap went to take the trash out and thought Michael had fallen asleep when he got back but Michael opened his sleepy eyes, looked up at Cap and asked in a low voice, "Cap, have you ever seen a ghost ship?" Cap stopped and looked down at the tired little boy who seemed to be serious with his question.

"I've heard things," Cap paused, deep in thought remembering lonely nights at sea, "on pitch black nights on dark waters that should be quiet, things I couldn't see, but was certain I could hear...aye, Michael." Cap turned and quietly poured some coffee into his cup, retrieved his bottle of Jack from a cabinet, grabbed what he called his "thinking cap" which was this old captain's hat he hadn't lost yet and carried it all up to the deck where he would drink and think and look at the stars. He was also wondering who this odd little boy was and where he came from.

Michael was asleep, when the former first mate, Willie, showed up to tell Cap about his new baby, Consuela, and he was ready to go back to work tomorrow. Cap invited him up on the deck and poured him a shot of whiskey and they both drank to Consuela. After a few minutes Willie asked him about how he got along by himself, and then Cap told him about Michael.

"Willie, the strangest thing happened. I was on the deck last night and I looked out across the water right out there," and he pointed towards the center of the deepest part of the ocean, "and I saw something but I wasn't sure what it was. I didn't think about it much but a little while later I looked again and I was beginning to be more certain that I was seeing something. It was swimming right towards the dock and it swam all the way up to the dock and climbed the ladder." Willie was frozen to his seat still holding his drink in his hand and listening intently to Cap's story. "It had a real pale complexion. I wasn't sure what it was while it was swimming but once it crawled up on the dock I saw it was a little boy, the strangest little boy you ever did see wearing the strangest looking little outfit you ever did see. Anyway he went over there and laid down behind the boathouse and I went over to see if he was all right. After talking to him, he seemed okay, so I let him stay on the boat here and he helped me out today. His name is Michael and he did a pretty good job. I ain't figured out who he is yet but he's a pretty bright little boy. He's got a lot to learn about shrimp boat fishing if that's what he wants to be. You come on in the morning and I'll just have him sit up here with me and watch you. I'll keep him out of your way and he can help out where he can." Willie said he was happy to have the help and said good night. "I'll see you in the morning, Willie."

"Ok, Cap," then Willie got up and headed home.

CHAPTER TWENTY

On a clear afternoon in December, Levi was sitting on his dock watching the tide come in and the sun go down when he saw a disturbance in the water. He immediately thought it was Michael. He was surprised, caught off guard and a little scared at first when a head popped up out of the water that he didn't recognize and then another. Levi didn't know what to say so he stood there quietly waiting for them to speak first. Finally one of them did. "Are you Levi?" the unusual looking boy asked.

"Yes," Levi answered.

"Do you know who I am," asked the stranger.

Levi looked at them and said, "I know Michael."

Jay said, "That's my brother and I'm trying to find him. Do you know where he is?"

"No, I haven't seen him in weeks," Levi answered.

"Neither have we and we've been looking for him this whole time," Jay explained.

"What do you mean looking for him? What happened?" Levi asked.

"No one knows," Jay answered.

Levi thought a second and asked, "Wasn't he in his supership? Does that mean you can't find his supership?"

"We did find his ship. He wasn't in it. We think he may have been captured or kidnapped or being held but we haven't seen or heard anything from him," Jay said.

I haven't either," Levi acknowledged.

"If you hear from him, tell him we're looking for him okay?" Jay asked.

"Okay I will," then Levi added. "What if I hear something? How can I contact you? Can you come back sometime and check?"

"Yeah okay," Jay said. Then Levi told Jay about the bottle that Michael and he used to pass notes to each other that was hidden under the dock in a cubby hole. Jay agreed he would be back in a few days. In the meantime, Levi said he would see if he could help figure out what happened to Michael.

As the two aliens were finishing up their story and getting ready to leave they assured Levi they would let him know if they found out anything. They said bye, got back into the water and boarded their supership. Levi watched the waves as the ship turned and headed back out of the creek. He looked up and saw Blackie, running toward him on the dock. Levi began talking to Blackie. "Hey boy," he greeted Blackie, "You missed all the action." Levi sat down on the dock, Blackie got up, walked over and lay down beside his feet and draped his tail across Levi's feet. Levi reached down, scratched his head and Blackie let out a little meow. Levi looked down at Blackie and said, "What do you think happened to Michael? How can he leave the supership? Where did he go?"

He reached down and patted Blackie's head. "It's okay, I'll catch you something to snack on." He picked up his shrimp net, straightened it out in his hands, slid his right hand through the loop of the rope and looped the rest like a lasso to hold, and then he picked up the net by the middle, lifting it high off the dock and then looped an edge of it over his index finger. Then he reached down with his left hand and grabbed the edge, lifted it up and separated his hands to open the net up as wide as he could before twisting his upper body and spinning around to toss the net out as far as possible. It opened up like a wobbly circle on the water. He saw it and realized that he was distracted. He was worried about Michael. You can't be distracted when casting a shrimp net. You have to focus and concentrate to do it right. He watched the net begin sinking out of sight. He let it sink for a few seconds before pulling it back in. It only had a couple of shrimp in it. He figured it was the activity of the supership that scared the little shrimp away for a few minutes. It didn't concern Blackie so he did what he always does. He jumped up and caught the two shrimp and held one down as he ate the other. Levi watched Blackie as he was trying to figure out where Michael could be. He looked down at Blackie and rubbed his head. "You love shrimp, don't you?" Levi walked to his house.

Before his visit by Jay, Levi had been anxiously preparing for his trip to Baltimore with his dad on Saturday morning. Now that he knew no one had seen Michael in several weeks he was concerned because it wasn't like Michael to disappear like this. It was completely out of character in Levi's mind. They were friends so Levi couldn't stop thinking about Michael.

Levi knew him a little now and to him, Michael loved everything. Levi remembered the day he and Michael rescued Abby and her family from being stranded on that deserted island. He had also helped Michael rescue a dolphin stuck across an oyster bed. He and Michael also stopped a bank from being robbed by dangerous alien criminals.

Michael loved Earth. He loved everything about it. He loved the oceans and he loved the sky, he loved the land, loved the people and loved the things that people had created. He loved potato chips and Mountain Dew. He loved everything so much that there's nothing he wouldn't do to help to protect these things. He didn't know it but he encapsulated everything good about humanity. There was one difference about Michael above all others, he wasn't human. Michael was from an alien species and through no fault of his own and like many coming from other countries to the US; he was born here to a family of illegal immigrants. That should give this baby an automatic citizenship card as a US citizen. He was a child of a family of refugees from another planet and I'd submit that it shouldn't matter as long as he was born here. It just happens to be that this family was the first of their species to migrate here to Earth from their doomed planet, Tyrol. If they landed in US waters, it could be true that Michael might be a US citizen. They really may not know that for a long time or at least until someone discovers the mothership buried in the ocean. Maybe then they could measure the distance to the ship and see if they're in US or international waters.

He was even more excited to see Abby now because he wanted to tell her about Michael. Eliza and her mom are coming as well as a lot of the other people who signed up to look for the castaways using Google Earth and were given an assigned space to search. It was the first time the lot of them were meeting so it was going to be great. They were all going to meet at the Baltimore Ravens stadium, right downtown and were all going to get great seats and maybe even meet some of the players. Later that evening after the game, a big dinner was being held for them all at the Marriot Downtown.

CHAPTER TWENTY-ONE

It was Saturday evening by the time of arrival at Baltimore-Washington International Airport, known as BWI. A representative from the hotel had been sent to pick them up and bring them to the Marriot in a hotel van. They were brought right up to the front door of the biggest hotel Levi had ever been inside of and it was downtown. When they walked into the lobby and went up to the registration desk Levi was taking it all in and was looking at everything. He thought it was massive and beautiful but also crowded and noisy. It was everything all at once. Once in his hotel room, he was excited to see that he could see the stadium from his window and it was all lit up. And the city lights and sounds were so mesmerizing he was constantly looking out. There were messages for them when they got to their rooms. Abby had left a message thanking everyone for coming and that they would all meet the next morning for breakfast and to get ready for the big game.

The next morning the young computer enthusiasts and their families from all over the country met in the lobby for the first time. Levi recognized a few names from his list and introduced himself to those and others. They were all excited to be here as they filled their plates at the free breakfast bar.

It was a cool Sunday in December and the Baltimore Ravens were playing at home against the Miami Dolphins. The Raven's sports broadcasters had been talking all week about the special presentations to be given out at half-time to the rescuers of the castaway football players. They talked to the Mortenson's and Maurice Munoz in interviews that were taped and excerpts were played throughout the week. The interviews always included Abby Mortenson, who set the entire possibility of a rescue in motion by placing a simple note on a small piece of torn paper inside a Coke bottle and tossing it out into the ocean. When asked what he thought about the castaway's rescue and Abby's efforts to be found, the Raven's coach stated, "Abby knew she was facing enormous odds but that didn't stop her from trying. She wanted to come home. She hoped they would be rescued and she did what she could to help make that happen. In the bigger picture, what she did was incredible. To maintain a constant struggle against enormous odds is the purest example of hope." He went on to explain how hope can be the all inclusive word for what a team does preparing for the next game. "For example, the team as a whole, hopes we win. To achieve that win, I hope we practiced the right plays and I hope my running back's knee holds out. Hope can hold an enormous burden, so in many cases, we try to influence the odds of getting what we hope for by preparation, considering different ideas, making a plan and working our plan. That's what increases the likelihood that what we hope for will happen. Hope is something Abby never ran out of and took actions to prove it." Each time, the names of Levi and Eliza were brought up as being the ones who found them, they also talked about the note in the bottle and how absolutely incredible it was, that it was found so quickly so far from where they were stranded. Everyone agreed it was an incredible story about this band of kids who had loosely formed a technically savvy organization, who came together for one reason, to help find this family.

The stadium was sold out on that Sunday afternoon. The temperature was in the 60s and the sky was blue. During halftime, all the students were led out onto the field to a makeshift podium and microphone. The presentation was going to be made on the field of the packed stadium. Eliza thought it was the coolest thing ever. The Mayor of Baltimore, Stephanie Rollins-Blake spoke first. She talked to everyone about what an excellent example of the power of teamwork, love for your fellow man and determination these students gave of themselves in this effort to find these members of our wonderful football family. It would be easier to find a needle in a haystack than to do what these young people did." The cheering continued.

The NFL GM, Rodger Goodell, spoke next and also lavished praises on the students, on the behalf of the National Football League, as he awarded each student official NFL Ravens and Dolphins jerseys, with their own names on the back and each also got a Certificate of Appreciation as Honorary Managers of the Ravens and Dolphins NFL teams, signed by the NFL General Manager and the Owner and Manager of each, the Ravens and Dolphins NFL teams. The crowd cheered as each individual was named and the students stepped forward. They were then asked to call out their names and say where they went to school. The crowd was encouraged to give a shout out each time the name of a school was mentioned. There was a big cheer that vibrated the stadium for every student's school. Levi, Abby, Eliza and all the rest were together with arms across each other's shoulders in a show of solidarity for their team of volunteers. After the ceremony, everybody went back to their seats to get ready for kickoff. It was a great day. The Ravens won the game, 24-20, and the joyful time continued. That evening a dinner was planned for the students and family members.

They met everyone on the Ravens' team at the dinner and many people they had never heard of. They had selfies taken with everybody. Maurice stood up, tapped on his glass to get everyone's attention and turned toward Abby. "Abby I want to personally thank you for being so brave and attempting against all odds to use every method for rescue." He went on to say, "I mean, we had a big white flag on top of the island the size of a sheet!" The crowd responded with a little laugh. Maurice was funny sometimes and Abby laughed too. Now that everyone was home safe and sound, they could look back at some of the humorous things that happened while they were there. "We had a stack of brush so big that if we ever did light it, you could have seen it from space." That brought another roaring cheer from the crowd. "We had this old flare that got wet in the boat. Both of us were afraid to strike it. We treated it like a live grenade." The crowd was laughing hard now. "That's okay, because we never had to use it," He looked at the students sitting at the dinner tables and said with all sincerity to the entire group, "At the Ravens organization we pride ourselves on our teamwork. That doesn't mean we hold each other up, which we do automatically anyway, but it means you have to bring something to the team that will make the team better with you than without you. That's what these guys did. They brought in a bunch of computer geniuses," everyone laughed, "and found a speck in the ocean," Maurice finished with, "Thanks to each and every one of you," then he sat down. A round of applause filled the room, and then Dan Mortensen stood up. He thanked the entire group just as Maurice did but added, "I won't ever be able to express my enormous gratitude and appreciation I feel toward all of you," he directed his comments to the kids. "You saved my life, but most of all, you saved my family's lives and for that I will be eternally grateful," he added as if it was an afterthought but tears began rolling down his cheeks and muffled laughter quickly stopped and the room became quiet. "I am grateful," he said again, speaking directly to the students. After a couple of seconds of silence, the crowd clapped loud and long. It was the first time Levi had stopped smiling in hours. He reached up and rubbed both cheeks up and down vigorously and pulled his smile down with his hands to relax his cheek muscles.

After he finished eating dinner, Levi looked over and saw Abby had finished her meal, too. He told his dad that he wanted to go say hi to her so he got up and walked to where she was standing after leaving her table. Abby started smiling, causing Levi to smile back when she saw him headed her way. Abby said, "Hey Levi, isn't this fun?"

"It's great, but I need to talk to you for a minute. Something bad has happened and you need to know about it." Abby knew by the look on Levi's face that it must be about Michael.

"What is it?" She asked.

"I was out on the dock just last week and Michael's brother showed up looking for Michael." Levi quickly began to tell Abby what he knew about what happened to Michael. "Abby! Something has happened to Michael."

"What happened? What happened to Michael?" She stopped and looked at him.

Levi continued, "Okay," he started over. "A couple of days ago I was sitting on the dock when I saw what I thought for sure was Michael's supership coming up the creek. I was half right. It was a supership but what surprised me was the head that came out of the water, it wasn't Michael. Then a second alien looking young person came out the other side. The first one got out quickly and asked me if I was Levi? I said, yes. He said he was Jay, Michael's brother," Levi told her.

"I know him," Abby said. "He helped rescue us off the island."

Levi continued, "The two came up on the dock. I couldn't believe I was talking to two more boys, alien-Earthling boys, I mean, like Michael. They were a lot like Michael, too. I mean, they looked a little like Michael but not exactly like him. Each one was different heights and stuff. The second boy then introduced himself as Mark. Jay said he was the one that chased after the bank robbers that were spotted by me and Michael that day in Savannah. And I did remember him, too," Levi smiled, "I remembered him but he looked different now. He said he came with Jay to see if he could help find Michael. They haven't seen him for weeks," Jay said. "I told them that I didn't know where he was either," Levi said, "I haven't seen him at all since he left for home after the Christmas Boat Parade. They said that they haven't either and were hoping I could help them find him. Of course I said sure." Then Levi asked Abby, "Do you think he's in Savannah, Abby?"

In deep thought she finally said, "I don't think so. Did they find his supership? " Abby asked, genuinely surprised.

"Oh, yeah, they said they found the supership in very deep water but he wasn't in it," Levi recalled.

"He wasn't in it? Where.... where could he go," Abby asked out loud. "He couldn't go far unless he went off with someone else," she continued. Then she thought of Michael getting caught and it scared her. Michael was always careful and getting caught was the thing that scared him most. She gasped, "Did they look around where they found the supership?"

"I don't know. I guess so," Levi assumed.

"I think he is somewhere else. I think maybe something bad has happened to him too," she hesitated for a moment, and then said, "We have to find him, Levi," as her face turned red and her eyes began to tear up.

"Wait just a second," Levi said. "Don't get upset. I know we need to find him. I've been thinking about it. That's what I wanted to talk to you about." Levi continued with his story. "I showed Jay where Michael and I would leave notes for each other under the dock. I told Jay that I would leave a note for him if we found him. That's what I said. If you come by, check here and if I hear something, I will leave you a note. If you hear something, you leave me a note."

"Okay, Levi," Abby said, "What's your plan?"

"This is as far as I've gotten,"Levi answered, "Telling you, I mean. I need you to help me make one."

"We can Google Earth search again," Abby offered.

"Yes, we can get started on that right away but we can't ask for any help. It would just be me and you," Levi said.

"My Mom knows about Michael. She might help," Abby added.

Then Eliza walked up to the two of them. "Hello guys, I've heard enough about football for one day. What are you guys talking about?" Levi and Abby both looked at Eliza at the same time then back at each other. They both knew they could use her help.

"Have a seat Eliza," Abby offered and Eliza sat between the two. Abby and Levi continued to talk around Eliza for a moment longer.

"We should have a meeting in our room upstairs when this is over," Levi suggested.

"I agree," Abby confirmed.

"We need to decide right now who else we should tell," Levi added and Abby agreed on that too. "Abby? This is the most important decision you are ever going to make," Levi said. Now Eliza was glued to Abby.

Abby quickly asked back, "Who else do you think we should tell?"

"I don't know," Levi said, "let's invite your mom to the meeting." Then they turned to Eliza. They both made Eliza promise to never tell anyone else what they are about to tell her unless we have another meeting like this first and all be in agreement. She was confused but said, okay.

Abby began, "Eliza, something incredible happened on that island that nobody knows about except me, Levi and mom. If we tell you, it will be four. We need to have an emergency meeting after we leave here and we will explain everything to you. If you can tell your mom that me and Levi invited you up to talk some more, maybe she will let you come alone."

"I'm sure she will. I have my phone," Eliza assured her.

"Good. Okay, I guess I should include my dad," Levi added.

"Me too," Abby said. Levi looked up at her and then she said, "He saved Dad too."

"Okay," Levi said and added, "everyone meet in my room when this is over." Everyone agreed.

Eliza left the impromptu meeting to go back and tell her mom that she had been invited to the Benjamin's room with Abby after dinner to hang out a little while. She smiled and said to keep her phone on and check the volume. Eliza checked her phone right then.

"Okay," her mom said. "Call me before you leave and have someone walk with you." Eliza assured her she would.

Helen walked over to Tony. "Look at the guys over there signing autographs for the kids," he told her. She looked at the ballplayers who had moved their plates away and started signing autographs for anyone who wanted one, on a ball or shirt and even a couple of helmets.

"They are all such nice people," she said, watching the kids who now feel like more than just fans but members of the team. She could see the excitement in the kid's eyes, as they high-fived and fake blocked each other each time they walked by each other or a player. He looked up and saw Abby across the room talking to Levi.

"They look like they are having a good time," Tony said but then did a double-take in their direction. He scrunched his eyes and scrutinized her with his sharp-focused gaze and could tell by her eyes, even from here that her demeanor had changed. "They must be having a serious conversation over there," he informed Helen of this observation. They watched Abby get up from her seat and walk their way. She came up to them with a serious look on her face.

"Is something wrong?" Helen asked.

"Mom, Levi invited us to his room after this. We need to talk about something," Abby said.

"What is it?" Helen asked.

"We will tell you there, okay?" Abby added.

"Okay, Abby," Helen said. Abby walked back toward Levi and Tony walked up to Helen.

"What was that all about," Tony asked.

"We have been invited to the Benjamin's room for a meeting. That's all I know," she said.

"Okay," Tony conceded but only because, for that amount of time, he felt like he could wait. He saw a team-mate walking up with a big grin on his face and turned to greet him. They immediately began talking about the great game and congratulated each other for their victory earlier.

As the evening wore on, the players started leaving individually and family members started going up to their rooms. Abby kept the small group together and they walked to the Benjamin's room. The adults all entered the room sharing small talk about the great day they've had. Dan then looked at Levi and asked, "So Levi, you said there was something you wanted to tell us?"

Levi turned to Abby, "Abby? Would you like to start the story?"

Abby was as nervous as she has ever been before. She knew that she had to be the one to tell it right so she stood up like she was at school. "Okay, so this is the way it all began," Abby started her story this way. She looked first at her mom, who stood motionless and expressionless; looking directly at her, and then she looked toward her dad whose look was more serious. She then looked over at Levi for his nod of encouragement which he obligingly gave with a supportive grin. "I'm so nervous, Levi. Can you help me say it?" Levi took a second and said,

"Okay, what do you want me to say?" he asked her. Then she gave him a sideways clue to what worried her.

"It's going to be alright don't you think?" Abby asked. Levi nodded yes. She started again, looking from Levi to Mr. Benjamin. He looked as confused as her dad. This was not going to be easy, she thought to herself. She was about to call the whole thing off, then she looked at her mother who gave her a reassuring smile. She decided to try again.

"Mommy," Abby began, "Michael is lost. We have to find him, don't we?" Helen looked at her daughter and her jaw dropped. Helen realized that what Abby just said was going to need a lot of explaining and was going to change the lives of the people in this room.

"Who is Michael?" Tony asked, more concerned than ever.

Abby looked at her dad. "Daddy, It all began one day while we were stuck on that island. There was a pool of water where I used to go and play around," she stopped again to think of how to just say it but she couldn't. "One day when I walked over there, there was a boy standing there by the pool," Abby managed to get out, almost in tears, before her father interrupted.

"What? There was somebody else there?" he couldn't hold back. He looked at Helen, "Did you know this?"

"No," she said as she shook her head, "Not at the time. Let Abby tell her story," Helen said. He turned back toward Abby and sat back down.

"Michael is my age, eleven, and he has very white skin. He had shorts on that day but no shirt on and his skin was all white. Oh, I forgot to tell you he was bald-headed too." She laughed a little when she said that. Everyone looked at Levi when they heard him laugh too, then they turned back toward Abby and continued to sit in silence, listening to Abby, as if they were watching a science fiction thriller. Abby went on, "He can speak English so we talked. He told me he lived there and when I asked where, he pointed to the ocean." A grunt sound came from Tony. Abby looked at her dad but continued her story. We have to find Michael, she reminded herself.

"Michael lives underwater in a spaceship," she managed to say.

"What!" Tony blurted out.

Helen said, "Tony it's true. You need to listen. There's a lot more."

"You're telling me we were on an island with aliens?" he asked.

"Not exactly," Abby answered. She began again, "No Daddy, Michael isn't an alien so stop saying that he is. He was born on Earth. His mommy and daddy are aliens."

Tony looked up at Abby a little embarrassed, and then he looked toward the others in the room and said, "I stand corrected. If Michael was born on Earth then he absolutely cannot be an alien."

Mr. Benjamin hadn't said a word and neither had Eliza. Abby continued, "Michael has a supership that he rides around in. He would ride it from his spaceship home to the island. I even drove it the day we were rescued."

Tony sprang up again as if to walk out of the room. He was ready to call this whole meeting off because he just couldn't accept any of it being true. He looked around the room to see how the others were taking it, and then back at Helen. She nodded at him and acknowledged that so far what Abby was saying was true, even Levi didn't disagree. Tony sat back down again. Abby went on with her story.

"I asked him if he would help us get home. He said that he would but I couldn't tell anyone and he had to stay out of sight. I wanted him to meet you but he couldn't. He was under strict rules that he wasn't supposed to be seen. I already had found the bottle and had put a note in it so I gave it to Michael and he brought it to Levi. Levi, do you want to take it from here?"

Levi looked surprised and said, "I didn't know about any of it. I just saw the bottle floating along and caught it in my casting net."

Tony asked, "But you know about him now?"

"Yes," Levi confirmed, "We're friends."

Tony looked at Helen again. She just gave him a little grin back and said, "I met him the last day we were there, Tony. Remember when I fell off the boat?"

Tony remembered, "Yes, you nearly scared me to death."

"I would have drowned except it was Michael who saved me," she confessed.

Tony was dumbfounded now and if he would have looked around the room, he would have seen all eyes were on Helen.

"He saved you?" Tony asked.

"Yes, believe it or not he does have what he calls his supership. It came from underneath me and pushed me up and out of the water at the last second. I was sure I was going to drown." She continued to look at Tony. "Then Michael, along with my brave Abby girl," she looked at Abby and smiled, "who jumped in to save me, came up out of the water beside me and I got to meet him." She looked at Tony and said, "They made me promise not to tell anyone about him." Tony did not look completely happy but had no idea what to say now. "Everything Abby is telling you is true. We both need to listen now." Helen looked toward Abby and told her to go on.

"Okay, Mommy." She looked around the room with a concerned look on her face, "Michael is missing and we have to find him. He helped us so we have to help find him." Abby looked at Eliza, "Will you help us, Eliza?"

"Yes," she answered quickly.

Abby looked around the room to each person and they all nodded in the affirmative. She felt good that she and Levi had picked the right people to tell, and then she looked at Levi for him to explain to everyone what they had come up with so far.

"Okay," Levi continued on with the plan. "The only thing we could think to do is to do what we did last time, use Google Earth. Since we can't tell anyone, it's up to just us to start the search. We do have an idea of where to start so that's better than before. Once we get back home, I will make a map of where his abandoned supership was found and then draw and assign a grid to everyone here toward the direction of the island where you were shipwrecked." Then he stopped talking and looked back at Abby.

"How do you know he is missing?" Tony asked.

"I can answer that," Levi answered. "His brother Jay came to our dock and told me." Dan looked down at Levi with an incredulous expression on his face like you might see on someone who just saw someone else's head suddenly turn purple. Dan was impressed that Levi was level-headed and totally believable in explaining his encounters with the Earthling-Aliens. "Last week I was sitting on our dock and I saw what I thought was Michael's supership coming up the creek. It was a supership but it was Michael's brother Jay and a friend of his. They were looking for Michael. I haven't seen him since the boat parade at Christmas but I told them that I'd help to find him and I showed him where to leave a note at our dock to keep in touch."

The group agreed to all pitch in and do what they could to help. The search for Michael would begin as soon as they got home. The meeting wound down after everyone decided they were too tired to keep talking and were ready to go to their rooms.

Tony and Helen closed the door to their bedroom when they got there. Abby knew that her dad wasn't happy that he had not been told about Michael. Helen was trying to explain that she had promised Abby and Michael that she wouldn't tell and she felt that it wasn't her place to tell such a secret.

"I wasn't even sure you would believe me. I don't have any proof," she said.

"Of course I would believe you after I examined you for a bump on the head," Tony quipped.

"See," Helen stated, "you would have been skeptical."

"Of course I would have been skeptical. That's why I should have met this little what-ever he is when Abby first met him. I don't know what else to say," Tony added.

"Tony, you know I nearly drowned out there. Michael saved me. He does have a supership and he did bring it up under me and lift me out of the water. Here's what I know. He's a cute little boy. He doesn't have any hair and his skin is almost white. He speaks English like you and me and he's very nice. Oh, and he did help us get rescued so we are going to help look for him, so don't say anything. We are all okay and now you know maybe the biggest secret of all time."

He asked, "That we are not alone? Yeah, that occurred to me." Then Tony just stood there for a second contemplating what he just said.

In Levi's room, his dad also had a few questions for Levi. "So you knew about this alien for how long now?" he asked.

The next day in the hotel lobby Levi saw a stack of Baltimore newspapers lying out. It had the biggest front page color picture of the packed football stadium Levi had ever seen. He could spot all the students too.

That same evening, back on a small island in the Bahamas, Michael was lying on his bunk in the belly of a shrimp boat when Cap turned the radio on. The news came on followed by the sports and told the scores of today's games including the Baltimore game. Baltimore beat Miami 24–20. Then the music started back, first playing another Christmas song, and the next song had a reggae beat. The steel drum beat filled the air and he started to sing a song he was making up about Abby. His ad libbed lyrics matched the beat of the drums and he began to sing quietly out loud. He sang;

"Abby would you like to ride
In my supership
We can go wherever you want to go.
We can run barefoot on an island
Or watch a penguin slide around in snow.

I want to see your list
Of all things beautiful
And see if your list matches mine
And if any of yours are different
I'll just add all those things to mine.

Then we can see everything together.
I'll even hold your hand if you don't care
Because all the Earth is worth exploring
If you'll only let me take you there

I hear Jamaican drums and voices in a rhyme
People up and dancing and the music's always fine
It makes me want to see you and we'll lose track of time
When I think of us together I see us laughing in my mind

"Oh no," Michael said. "I didn't just make that up in my head
did I? I better not do that in front of Jay. He would kill me."

CHAPTER TWENTY-TWO

The next day Michael grew anxious when Willie showed up. Michael didn't know he was coming and nearly jumped off the boat to run away but the look on his face didn't seem threatening. Then he greeted Michael with a thick Jamaican accent, "Hola, Michael! You can call me, Willie. Cap told me you were here. You helped him out yesterday?" he asked, nodding his head and grinning".

"Yes," Michael answered.

"Cap said you want to be a great fisherman, like him?" He went on with a big open smile.

"That would be great," Michael said, starting to grin back, returning Willie's infectious smile. He knew he wasn't in any danger with Cap here. Then Michael remembered to congratulate him on his new baby. Willie extended an invitation to Michael.

"Michael...you absolutely have to come see the most beautiful baby girl ever born, now don't you?" he said with his head tilting to reflect in a totally serious but humble way.

"Sure Willie, I'd like to meet her!" Michael quickly answered back.

"Tonight then, when we get back, you can come with me and meet my Consuela," he said with his heavy Jamaican accent. His hair was in dreadlocks and he wore an old dirty Marlins baseball cap over it sometimes to keep the sun out of his eyes.

Then Willie turned to Cap, "Hola, Cap!"

"Good morning, Willie. Let's get going!" Cap grunted back.

Willie reached down and started checking the nets again, then the rigging. Michael watched the two men working together, pointing things out to each other and picking up speed as they were readying to shove off. Once out in the fishing area, he and Willie worked together with Michael matching every move Willie made. Willie felt like Michael was doing a good job helping and slapped him on the back once the first haul was in the hole. Michael saw he was still smiling and began to wonder if Willie was always like this.

They had an even better day and were able to make an additional run with Willie and Michael there. Cap was pleased with the day's work and gave Willie a little extra money to buy Consuela a fish mobile for her crib. He chose to stay at the boat when invited to come along with the two of them but Michael went to meet Willie's newest addition, like he promised. Michael had never seen a human baby as young as Consuela. They stopped at the market where Cap had spotted the fish mobile earlier and gave Willie the money to buy it. When he got to Willie's apartment he met Willie's wife. She had the darkest most beautiful brown skin with a totally jet black head full of hair but she was the tiniest thing he had ever seen. "Would you like to hold her?" Willie asked.

"Oh no," Michael said, afraid he might hurt the frail looking baby if she started squirming or something.

Willie handed the box with the mobile in it to his wife and said, "This is from Cap."

She smiled and told him to thank Cap and she opened the box containing the colorful fish mobile with different bright colored fish hanging down and mounted it on the edge of Consuela's bassinet. She wound up the music box part and the mobile started turning and playing, Rock-a-bye Baby.

"Okay, she's going to love that," Willie said and sat down in a chair at their table with Consuela in his lap and he and Michael began making goo-goo eyes at her to get her to smile.

Michael laughed when she smiled at him. "She's smiling at me," he said.

"She likes you," Willie said.

Michael thought to himself, that this is exactly what his family does to babies. That helped him to relax a little and then he got close up while Willie held little Consuela, he reached down to touch her hand and smiled big when she held onto his finger and looked right at him.

"Look, she's grinning big. See, I told you she likes you, Michael," Willie said.

Michael soon headed back to the boat in a good mood and told Cap about the cute baby before heading to his bunk. Michael continued on as the days passed living and working on the boat with Cap and Willie. Willie was great and he taught Michael everything about shrimping. He never said anything about how odd Michael looked. He even invited him and Cap to his house for Christmas dinner which Willie's wife made. It was some kind of seafood stew called bouillabaisse that had every kind of seafood you could find around here in it, including, fish, crab, shrimp, scallops and oysters and Michael thought it was great! The cooler winter months were quieter times after hurricane season ended.

The shorter days passed quickly during the cooler winter months, hurricane season ended and February came quickly as well once they started fishing everyday but after work Michael was becoming more anxious to get home. Cap had told him he would be leaving to go back to Charleston when he could hope to get three or four days of good weather in a row. Michael was excited to be going back but still a little nervous. He still had no idea how to get in touch with anyone. He had no phone numbers, no address as if he could get to a phone anyway. He was going to have to wait until somebody came to him or he found a way to get home even when he got to Charleston. What would Abby do, he kept asking himself. Michael pondered these thoughts while in his mind's eye he remembered Abby's face always smiling at him. He remembered her and every detail. He wondered if she remembered him. He never thought about growing up too much and falling in love but his chest hurt when he thought of her and he was sad that he couldn't see her again. He got up off his bunk, went up to the deck, sat down, looked up at the stars and wondered, what Abby would do? He stood up again and walked to the edge of the railing, looked out across the water, and then he looked down across the beach. He saw a Coke bottle someone had left behind, lying on the beach. Levi had planted the idea about how bad trash was. He remembered what Levi told him about keeping his area clean. If that had not been Levi's way he would never have found Abby's bottle. So, he climbed down the dock and jumped down to the soft warm sand, walked to the bottle, picked it up and looked at it. The lid was missing and it was full of sand and water. There was a trash can a little bit farther down so he walked there and threw the bottle in the can and started walking along the beach. He picked up a fat piece of driftwood and started dragging it behind him, scratching a big wavy line into the sand, pulling it along, making lines and circles.

He came across a nice, untouched and pristine part of the beach. He looked back at the deep depression he had made dragging the big stick. Then he began dragging his piece of driftwood again but this time began drawing letters about 20 ft. long spelling out the name Abby. He stood back, looked at it, walked down about a hundred steps and spelled out Abby, again. Then he walked down about a hundred steps and spelled her name out a third time. He began to sing a little song he made up about her as he walked along dragging the stick behind. He knew Valentine's Day was tomorrow. He was sad because he had hoped to somehow talk to her. Then he began making up a little song:

If a rose can bloom in the desert
And a daisy can bloom in the snow
Both of these flowers so different,
But both have the same will to grow

It's not a big deal and it's silly

How much kids like to play,
But I'd like you to be my Valentine
Just because it's Valentine's Day.

Please won't you be my Valentine,
Please be mine, please be mine.
Please won't you be my Valentine, Abby
Because it's Valentine's Day.

After a while, with tears in his eyes, Michael laid the stick down and walked back to the dock.

CHAPTER TWENTY-THREE

Christmas and New Year's holidays passed and Levi had almost given up hope. So far none of them had even found a clue to Michael's whereabouts. There was no evidence to suggest where Michael might be and school stuff took up most every day now.

Eliza was busier than ever too but she was not giving up. She had found the island that Abby and her family were stranded on and she knew she could find Michael. She was going to look and look again. She spent more time than anyone else looking for him.

February 15th, the day after Valentine's Day, Eliza was sitting at her computer, zooming in on islands and waters off the Atlantic seaboard for any sign of Michael. She took a break and was sitting there looking at some of the news articles that were scrolling past her. Suddenly, she sees a headline that catches her attention. The headline read, "Who is Abby?" and she zoomed in on the picture. There was an image of a long string of very large letters spelling out the name Abby over and over scrawled on a sandy beach on an island. The story was presented as a mystery. Who is Abby and who was drawing these letters? It's being speculated that a lost love could be a motive. The pictures and accompanying story online have drawn over 50k likes. One poet even wrote a poem titled, "Abby". It went,

"Abby, Abby, Abby,
Hear My Cry
I pray the tide

Will bring you back
Before I die."

Then a thought came to her mind. Could Michael have done this? It occurred to Eliza that this could be what they're looking for and she immediately forwarded the story by email to Abby. Abby had been searching her assigned area every day for an hour and sometimes longer. Michael was still missing and she needed to help find him. He had helped her so she was determined that she was going to keep searching, like Levi and Eliza, until we find him.

Her mother was very supportive and concerned for Michael's safety and kept her eye out for news articles that may indicate someone fitting Michael's description having been found. After perusing hundreds of news articles, she saw no suggestion of anyone like Michael being found dead or alive and that gave her hope.

Suddenly Abby came running through the house to her mother, calling her. "Mommy, Mommy, Mommy!"

"I'm in here, Abby. What's wrong?" Abby ran to where her mother was and while crying, she fell into her arms.

"Mommy, Mommy, it's Michael. It's Michael. Michael is sending me a message!" Through the tears, she said, "We found Michael!" she said again. Failing to speak coherently, Helen did not understand what Abby was saying.

"Okay, okay, slow down. What do you mean you found Michael?"

"Mommy come look. I have to show you." Helen got up and followed Abby into her bedroom to her computer. She was looking at a photograph taken from a helicopter of a beach and the name Abby was clearly written in large printed letters over and over along the sandy stretch of beach.

Helen looked at it and looked at Abby and asked, "Are you sure?"

"I know it is. I just know it. We have to do something Mommy. We have to do something, Michael needs me. He's calling me. He's lost and he needs me. He wants to be found. I've got to go find him," she cried.

Helen began a hard conversation after a moment of thought. "I don't know what to say this minute. Let me think about it a little while and talk to you father."

"Mommy, Mommy, we've got to go find him," she cried in her arms and got up from her mother and ran to her bed. She lay there crying into her pillow.

Helen got up, went to her little girl and put her arm across Abby's shoulders and asked, "Does Levi know?"

Abby stopped crying for a moment and sat up sniffing back her runny nose. She said that she didn't know, so her mother suggested they forward the article to Levi and get his ideas on what they should do next. So, for the moment Abby was happy to do just that. It was someplace to start. She jumped up, wiped the tears from her face and immediately forwarded the article to Levi's e-mail. He was sitting at his computer screen when he saw the message come up from Abby.

He was excited to see it was from Abby and went straight to open it. He was more surprised to see the name "Abby" written in the sand on the beach in the attached news article she sent along. He definitely could read the name Abby on the beach and he began to think about that. Was it possible this could be Michael reaching out? He already knew it had to be something different that Michael would have to do to get a message to them. It was the only clue so far, so he thought it was worth investigating. He wanted to try to pinpoint this island on his map. The news article had the name of the island and a little map of the island. He printed out a picture of the map and put an "X" on the island where the photograph was taken of the beach with the name Abby written on it. He put both in an envelope then ran down to the dock to hide it where Jay knew where to look the next time he came by.

The next day was Saturday so Levi got up and ate a quick breakfast with his Dad. He told his dad about Eliza's discovery and they are going to check it out.

"That sounds like a long shot, but good luck," Dan said.

"Yeah, I put a note and a map where that island is in my bottle and left it for Jay at the dock. I'm going to hang around the dock today and see if he comes by," Levi stated.

After he finished, he jumped up and ran out the door, slamming it behind him. Blackie was lying on a patio chair. "Come on, boy. Let's go fishing," he called. Blackie slowly stretched before hopping down to the floor and trotting over to Levi following closely at his feet. Levi went to the utility room and collected his casting net and fishing rod, closed the door and headed for the dock. He looked and saw that his note he put in the cubby hole was still there. Jay hadn't been by yet.

Levi decided he would just stay out here for a while. He pulled up the first crab basket to check it. There were a couple of blue crabs in it. The other only had one. He threw them back in. Then he picked up his shrimp net and looped the rope and picked up the net and prepared to throw it. He stood on the edge of the dock and gave the net a smooth toss. It opened up over the water and settled down out of sight. Blackie got up and moved closer. Levi began to pull the net in. He pulled in two little shrimp but that was enough for Blackie. He pounced and got them both.

He readied his net for another toss. He stood on the edge of the dock again and looked out across the creek. A turbulent tide caught his attention and he started staring. Then he saw the familiar top of a supership coming up out of the water. He waited to see who was going to get out of it. It was Jay. Levi waved at the supership and indicated that it was okay to come up on the dock.

As Jay was climbing onto the dock, Levi retrieved the note and map he had put in the cubby hole the day before.

"Hey Jay, I'm glad you came today. I think we found a clue," Levi said.

CHAPTER TWENTY-FOUR

It was a busy weekend on the waters of the Bahamas as Cap and Michael got an early start and headed out on the way to Charleston. Further south a USCG patrol boat picked up a radar hit of a bogey traveling faster than anything else on his screen. Capt. Collevechio was free and clear to investigate this anomaly now that he had a fix on its position. He decided to set his course to intercept the bogey's course. He wanted to see where it's going or maybe he could catch up to it. He gave the command.

Jay was cruising up to the island where the name Abby had been scrawled on the beach and it was where they suspected Michael was stranded. They looked for a big beach and found several. Finally they came up to one near a dock.

"I don't see anything, do you?" Jay asked Levi who had decided to come along in case he was needed.

"No. Let me out. I'll go look around," Levi offered.

Jay pulled up next to a dock ladder. Levi got out of the supership and climbed up to the dock. He looked in the boathouse but no one was around. Out back he saw a dirt road and a few buildings further down and a small grocery store. He headed in that direction.

Only about two hours behind them now, Capt. Collevechio was bearing down on the target. The radar man had momentarily lost the bogey at the island but he was certain he hadn't seen it leave. The Coast Guard Captain continued on this same heading.

Levi walked down to the store, opened the screen and walked in. It was old and dusty but it was cool inside and had most things.

He walked over and grabbed a Mountain Dew out of the cooler and walked up to the storekeeper to pay for it.

"Excuse me but I'm looking for someone. He's about my age and size. He has really light skin and a bald head."

"No, Mon, I don't know nobody like that," the cashier said as he gave Levi his change.

"Thanks," he said as he turned to leave.

A voice came from behind him. "Are you talking about Michael?" Willie asked.

"Yes!" Levi said louder as he turned around.

"Yes, I know Michael. He worked on the shrimp boat with Cap. They are gone already. Left early this morning before sun up to go back to the mainland," Willie said.

Levi was confused and asked Willie, "Where did they go?"

"Cap goes to Charleston when he's not here," Willie answered.

"So you're saying that Michael is on a shrimp boat heading to Charleston right now?" Levi clarified.

"Yes, that's right, they left early today," Willie confirmed.

"Okay thanks," he said and ran out the door headed back to the dock where Jay and his supership was waiting for him.

"Did you find Michael?" Jay asked.

"I found someone who knows him and they said he's on a shrimp boat heading to Charleston. They left this morning," Levi explained.

"I bet we can catch them," Jay said as he turned his supership around and set a course for Charleston.

Still on the same course heading toward an island, Capt. Collevechio was more curious now. The bogey goes to islands and becomes lost in the shoreline. He had never been able to figure out what these things are and he wasn't ready to give up just yet.

At that moment, the radar man spoke up. "Bogey sighted," he said. Capt. Collevechio walked over to see for himself what the radar man was seeing. He could tell that the blip on the screen was moving away from the island waters and heading northwest now. The captain plotted his own course. If the bogey maintains this heading they would be able to intercept whatever this is way sooner than he expected. He gave the new heading and increased their speed. He was gaining ground.

Out on the ocean, heading to Charleston, Cap and Michael were cruising along and making good time on the calm seas. Michael walked up to stand beside Cap. "I bet your folks are going to be happy to see you, huh Michael?"

"Yeah, I can't wait to get home. I can tell them I'm going to be a shrimp boat captain one day," he said.

Cap grinned at the boy. "So you got the fever now, do you? You want to have your own boat?"

"That would be awesome," he said as he looked out ahead at the blue with white capped waves blending in with the blues of the horizon. He could get used to this, he had already decided.

In a supership closing in on the much slower shrimp boat, Jay and Levi spotted a bogey of their own on Jay's radar. "Looks like this might be it up ahead," he told Levi. "Uh oh," we have a visitor," Jay relayed to Levi, "It looks like our old friend from the US Coast Guard."

Jay decided what he wanted to do to get their attention. He told Levi to hang on. He speeded up his supership and caught up to the shrimp boat but he couldn't get the crew's attention so he decided to lay back a little to decide what to do next.

In the meantime, the Coast Guard ship was catching up as well. Cap spotted the Coast Guard vessel closing in on an intercept course but still a ways away.

As the Coast Guard ship got closer, the captain could see, using his binoculars, there was only a crew of two on board. He maintained his speed.

"I wonder what they are looking for?" Cap asked Michael rhetorically.

"Who is it?" Michael asked.

"Looks like the Coast Guard to me. I wonder what they want?" Cap asked, again.

That's when Michael began to look concerned. He didn't know what he was going to say if they asked him who he was.

In a move of desperation, Jay pulled up alongside the shrimp boat to be able to see the cabin. Both passengers were looking straight ahead and occasionally at the Coast Guard vessel that was closing in.

Jay tried again on the side where Michael was standing. He matched the speed of the boat and came to the surface like a dolphin would do. Then out of the corner of his eye, Michael saw a reflection in the water beside them. He recognized the supership's silhouette right away. At the same time, the Coast Guard vessel called for the shrimp boat to stop for inspection boarding.

Michael looked at Cap and said, "Cap, my family has found me. I need to leave now." He quickly shed his coveralls and cap and left them on the deck as he climbed over the side of the boat and leaped out into the water on the opposite side where the Coast Guard ship was approaching. "I'll see you in Charleston," he yelled as he dove underwater.

Cap turned back to look at the Coast Guard ship pulling closer. He heard a noise and turned around as another little boy was climbing over the rail and getting back on his boat. The boy was soaked when he looked up and saw Cap looking at him. Cap pointed with a nod of his head at the clothes Michael just took off. Levi saw them and started dressing quickly as the Coast Guard ship pulled up close.

"Is everything okay, Captain," Cap called out to the officer.

The captain and a couple of armed crew members jumped onto the shrimp boat and started looking for any kind of contraband while Capt. Collevechio talked to Cap.

The captain looked toward Levi who gave a little wave toward the officer and his crew, and then he checked Cap's registration and asked about the boy. "Who's the boy?" he asked Cap.

"I'm Levi," Levi said.

"That's my crew," Cap said, "We're heading to Charleston."

"Have you seen any other boats or anything close to the surface out here?" the captain asked.

"No, Captain, ain't nobody out here but me and my mate," Cap said.

Not wanting to waste any time, the captain returned to his ship. The bogey was gone. He turned his big ship around and headed southwest to continue patrolling the sea.

After a few minutes when the military vessel was out of sight, a small sub came up near the shrimp boat. Michael got out, swam to the boat and climbed a ladder back onboard the shrimp boat. Cap and Levi both saw him.

"Hey Levi," said Michael, "you found me."

"Hey Michael," Levi said, "Eliza found the note you left."

"What note?" Now Michael was really confused.

"You wrote Abby's name on the beach back there, didn't you?" Levi asked.

"Yes… You found me because I did that?" Michael asked.

"Eliza did," he reiterated, giving Eliza all the credit.

He turned to Cap and said, "I will come see you in Charleston, Cap."

"I'd like that Michael," Cap said.

Then Michael turned to Levi and asked, "Are you ready to go home?"

"Yeah," Levi said.

"Okay, let's go," Michael said and they both jumped off the boat. Cap walked over and looked out but he could see nothing, so he returned to the wheelhouse and started heading toward Charleston again.

It only took a short time for the supership to pull up to Levi's dock. He told Michael goodbye and to come see him. He said he would come by Saturday.

As soon as Levi got inside, he started calling for his dad. "Dad, Dad?" he called. Then he ran to his room, got on his computer and emailed Abby and Eliza. He typed: We did it!

Dan walked in from the kitchen and asked, "How'd it go?"

"We found him, Dad. We found him. He was on a shrimp boat in the middle of the ocean and we found him. He's on his way home now," Levi said.

"That's great, Levi. Good job," Dan said.

Abby messaged back how happy she was and Eliza e-mailed back that she couldn't believe it. Levi told them that Michael was fine and that he was probably getting home about now and he said he would come over next Saturday.

Jay and Michael made it back to Atlantis where a jubilant mother was waiting for him. A big party with cake and ice cream was also waiting for him and his friends.

At the party, Michael told them all about the Russian sub and then about getting stranded on an island and getting a job on a shrimp boat, and he told them all about Cap and Levi. He couldn't believe how many people were worried about him. He was happy to be home.

CHAPTER TWENTY-FIVE

Next Saturday morning was warmer when Michael drove his supership to Levi's dock. Michael said that they had recovered his supership and brought it back to Atlantis and had it repaired. "It's as good as new now." Michael said. Levi had his fishing pole out and was fishing. He handed it to Michael as he picked up his casting net to try to catch a snack for Blackie who had come to join them.

After catching a few shrimp for Blackie, the two boys sat down on the dock with their feet hanging over the side. The tide was too low for their feet to touch the water so they were just watching all the fish, shrimp and schools of smaller fish scooting quickly across the surface as other fish chased them.

Levi looked up into the sky and asked Michael, "At night, can you see your planet from here?"

"You can see Betelgeuse from here," Michael answered. "That's our star."

"I know where Betelgeuse is. It's the highest star in the Orion constellation," Levi said.

Michael said, "Yeah, it took forever to get here."

Levi asked, "Do you think the Air Force would have shot your spaceship down if they had seen it?"

"That would have been crazy! Can you imagine that happening? They couldn't have anyway. We were already crashing." Michael said smiling. "But, if we weren't crashing you mean? So here's the scenario as I see it." Michael began. "Another planet has to evacuate with a population of families, like us, not warriors and they don't want to die, so maybe they have a powerful weapon or even a nuclear weapon and they think they can use that to bully another planet to let them land and take over. Well, that's not enough to defeat Earth. We not only have nuclear weapons but we also have a much larger quantity and we have the mechanism to take the battle to space so they better play nice or as soon as they expose their nefarious motives, we can send the Transformers after them. We have enough intercontinental missiles to stop them before they could ever disperse microbes or contaminate drinking water. How can they possibly build an interstellar spaceship that can also withstand a nuclear explosion? I ain't buying it," Michael said, "It's a joke, propaganda." Levi listened, never really having given it much thought until now.

Michael had told Levi some of this story but now he was learning more. Michael said that Tyrol was a planet from the solar system that orbited the star Betelgeuse. Levi knew Betelgeuse was easy to spot because it could be seen in the night sky as part of the constellation Orion. Its position in this constellation is the uppermost star on the left side. Michael had explained that Betelgeuse was a dying star and where once it was the 10th brightest star in the night sky, now it's no brighter than others in the Orion constellation. Levi had not noticed that. He said it is in the midst of becoming a red giant and as it became larger it began to heat up Tyrol and as the temperature began to rise, water on the planet began to dry up. It became pretty clear to the inhabitants of Tyrol that in order to survive they would have to abandon their home for another planet. They began to search the stars in a desperate attempt to find a planet with an environment that contained water and breathable air. It had to be out there somewhere. After hundreds of years searching the universe they heard a signal. They detected a signal, something they had never heard before from the Milky Way galaxy. They headed in the direction of the sound and as they got closer, do you know what it was they heard?" Michael asked.

"What?" Levi asked.

"Music, they heard music," Michael continued. "We learned your English so much quicker because of all the songs and then the radio shows that were being broadcast across space. We lived your past this way and now it's how we live our present. We just continue to observe everything like we did from space only now we are here underwater," Michael concluded.

"Michael?" Levi asked. "Do you think there are any more planets with people like us on them? Any more intelligent aliens?"

Michael began like this, "Look at Earth. Earth is inhabited by thousands of species. Some of those species are intelligent and we can watch as they interact with each other, like ants, but we don't see ants using shovels and buckets. And on top of that, they act like they don't see us until we start chasing them. Could you imagine giants walking around on Earth so large and so different looking that they would just ignore us. We see elephants, the largest creature that walks around on Earth being led around circus tents like pets. We don't see whales, pulling barges across the ocean. We don't see any animals that smart. Not gorillas or chimpanzees even though we say they are smart enough to learn a language, but not smart enough to build a school. It's just humans that do that. So, even if we find a planet or moon with thousands of species of life including bacteria, fungi, insects, reptiles and mammals on it, it still doesn't mean there's intelligent life. So far we haven't found any jungle planets. We know there were two, Tyrol and Earth, but now we are back to one again because we all live here on Earth now."

"I guess you're right, Michael," Levi said, "but, that's probably a good thing."

"Why is that a good thing?" Michael asked.

"You know, Michael, a lot of people are afraid of aliens and they don't even know if there are such things," Levi answered.

"What are they afraid of?" Michael asked.

Levi continued, "They're afraid they are going to invade Earth and destroy us or make slaves out of us or even eat us."

"That's ridiculous," Michael pushed back. "Earth has over 6

billion people on it. There is no way any alien force could ever do that. They couldn't bring enough stuff with them to do much of anything. Aliens would understand this before attacking. They aren't just going to be riding in guns a-blazing like the James Gang. Earth was ready to defend itself even back when we got here, but now look what we have. We have nuclear weapons, missiles and missiles with nuclear weapons. I don't believe even a lot of spaceships could survive very long. Just look at how many we have and we can send them in from all directions. So if they want to invade us, just come on, we still have more. I heard that everybody has a gun in the US, that there are more guns than toothbrushes. If someone doesn't have one then the person next door probably has two. I just can't see being invaded by a spaceship from another planet, not possible. What kind of weapons could they possibly have that we don't, laser weapons? Sorry, we got those too. And if they could destroy the whole world at one time, what would be the point of that?"

"That's true," Levi said, "We are not defenseless. We're loaded with weapons of all kinds. Any alien invasion may threaten but I bet they would be surprised at our arsenal."

Michael then said, "If they do come to Earth, their only option is to gradually infiltrate the communities and remain undetected the entire time because now we have a Space Force of our own."

Levi picked up on what Michael said. It was the clearest statement that Levi ever heard Michael say that he thought of himself as one of us.

Michael continued, "We have the weapons already. We can deliver them into space already, too. Any invasion would have to be overwhelming. Any overwhelming size force would easily be detected far enough in advance for defense preparation and the US could meet them in space long before they reach Earth." Michael opined further, "In my opinion, the likelihood of Earth being invaded by an alien army is highly unlikely or doomed for failure. The earth is fully capable of defending itself. Imagine how large an alien force would have to be to overwhelm earth. 100 motherships,

1000 motherships, it would still not be enough. The best it could hope for is to come in undetected and infiltrate our society over generations, like we did. We couldn't even do what we did today without being detected long before we reached Earth with all the sophisticated telescopes everywhere now."

Levi listened to what Michael was saying. He had never heard it put this way before. Michael continued, "It is more likely that an alien arrival here would be one of scientific exploration, immigrants or refugees and not an invasion force. Any aggressive invaders would run out of weapons long before they made any major impact on Earth and any invading army would be overwhelmed and defeated."

Then Michael surprised him by quoting from a president.

"Like President Franklin Roosevelt said," Michael said proudly, "The only thing we have to fear is fear itself. However you look at it, if we attack an invading force before they reach Earth, any atomic blast should destroy them or at least send them cartwheeling across the universe from now on. Have you seen an atomic blast? Can you even imagine how far it could knock someone away from us in SPACE? But doing that means we may destroy an entire race of refugees. Anyway, whatever large size ship they arrive on would be the mothership and would be holding all the groups of refugees and valuables including women, children and the elderly. If they manage to reach Earth, I doubt they would want war. If they do, I'm pretty sure we are fully capable of taking them out with overwhelming force before they reach the surface. If that failed, my strategy would be, bring them down to Earth. Bring them to the ground. We can take care of them even quicker there. We have tanks with missiles now and we can surround them like the Bolivian army surrounded Butch Cassidy and the Sundance Kid. It would be time to play the last song of this movie, too, because it would be over." Michael finished.

Levi added his thoughts that he hadn't really considered until now, "Yeah, fear is the worst. You just don't know what's going to happen. But after meeting you, you aren't so scary."

"Yeah, but I scared Abby!" he said, and they both started laughing.

Levi was sure that Michael wouldn't be afraid of aliens. Michael continued, "I don't think they would want to destroy Earth or take over Earth, just the opposite, they most likely would just want to live here, to move into a neighborhood. The aliens would not likely have any reason or means to mount a large-scale attack to attack the entire planet Earth. They maybe could bluff and get away with it for a while but when the fight begins, the weapons of the United States alone could eliminate the alien threat very quickly. No alien spaceships would come in from across the universe ready to battle a Space Force." Levi was sure they probably would not be expecting that.

Michael added, "Even our mothership had no weapons of any capacity to invade a planet, and a force field would have been a nice accessory but it didn't have one," he said. "Our invading force consisted of a mothership and about 100 smaller ships with defensive weapons and small arms, so any attempt to attack Earth would have been disastrous for us. The only defense we had was the maneuverability of the superships. We could avoid being shot down but were confined to strictly defensive maneuvers. Our offensive weapons were limited to minor level EMF producing lasers on some superships. These might be able to interfere with the operation of aircraft but they have never tried it because it hasn't been necessary. Anyway, then they may find us and the quantity of aircraft that would be unleashed on us would quickly eliminate our mothership and the small number of aircraft we have. The battle would end quickly with US forces overwhelming everything. I think that's why alien spaceships have never threatened Earth...if there are any."

Levi was a little surprised, "So you think that there might be other alien races out there that know we are here but know they couldn't beat us in a war anyway?"

"No way could they," Michael stated, "We could surround them in no time and they would be surrendering before they could say," then Michael changed his voice to sound like Marvin the Martian and said, "Take me to your leader." Levi laughed at that.

Levi listened to Michael's thought out theory about an invading alien army and then asked Michael, "Okay, what if they have superpowers like Superman?"

Michael looked at him, "It's funny you should say that because I was told that when they picked up the Superman TV show and learned that Superman was from a solar system with a red sun and well, Tyrol has a red sun, Betelgeuse, so rumors started that maybe we would all have superpowers when we got here."

"I guess you didn't then?" Levi asked.

"Nope, no x-ray vision or anything," Michael answered.

"That must have been disappointing. Well, it's a good thing you landed here then," Levi said, "You could have landed where the Klingons live."

Michael caught on quickly to the Star Trek reference. "The Klingons would have been bad!" Michael agreed and added, "What if we had gotten attacked by Darth Vader's evil empire?"

"You'd be toast! You'd have to wait on Luke Skywalker to rescue you!" Levi said excitedly.

"No way would I wait. I'd take my own light-saber and cut Darth Vader's hand off like he did to Luke Skywalker," Michael said, "Then, I'd steal an Imperial Galactic Ship and get away."

Levi was certain Michael would do just that.

The two boy's friendship deepened as they picked up their exciting expeditions where they left off before Michael went missing, taking trips to islands and sometimes just spending time with Blackie fishing off the dock.

On the first of May Levi got an email from Eliza Martinez. It was an invitation to her Indian Princess's Club weekend event at Ft. McAllister on the Ogeechee River. The email said,

Hi Levi,

I was asked by the Park Ranger, Mr. Brown, who has a daughter in the Indian Princess's Club, if I could show them how we rescued the Mortenson's and Mr. Munoz. I was wondering if you would come help me show them how you did your part and then I could show them how I did my part if you aren't too busy. When I asked the Park Ranger, he said that it was a great idea. So, can you come?

Eliza

Levi knew where the park was and said he thought it would be fun. He showed his Dad the invitation from Eliza and his Dad was more excited than he was. Although he and his dad were close, most of the things they did together were spontaneous. It was rare they planned things like this together. They had a few laptop computers they could use and show everyone how they were able to get online and Google Earth to locate the island.

Okay, Levi agreed and sent his acceptance note back telling Eliza that he would come. "Is it okay if I bring a friend?" Levi asked back.

"Sure," Eliza responded. His dad had thought it was a great idea and agreed to take him.

After Eliza invited Levi to the event, he ran out to the dock and left a note for Michael. He wanted Michael to come along. When Michael heard that he had been invited, he quickly answered yes.

On the day of the event, they exited I-95 to state highway 144. They stayed straight for several miles before turning off highway 144 and entering the gate of the park. The ranger's permanent residence was on his left going into the wooded area. Large ancient looking trees with bent and twisted limbs were everywhere and made bright leafy green canopies that cast shade over large areas of the park. Once inside the gated area of the old fort, there didn't seem to be much to it. There weren't any walls at all, only a few, neatly kept rustic log buildings could be seen.

The park rangers here like to do lots of events for young people to enjoy. They schedule a lot of fun activities for families plus it has a museum. Folks like to donate locally found artifacts to the museum from an era that didn't seem so long ago, especially when you stand under these century old trees with Spanish moss draping to the ground in places like Christmas tree icicles.

When Levi and Michael arrived at Fort McAllister, the two boys were excited to see Eliza. They jumped out of the car as soon as it stopped when they saw her walking in the area next to where the cars were parking and ran to her.

"Eliza!" Levi called.

Eliza heard her name and stopped when she saw the two boys running her way.

"Hey Eliza," Levi said.

"Hey Levi," then she turned to the other boy who was the same size as Levi but with much lighter skin and a baseball cap on his head

"Eliza?" Levi said, "This is Michael."

"Hi Eliza," Michael said. "Thanks for inviting me."

"Hey Michael, it's nice to meet you finally," she said with a big grin.

The Civil War fort bordered the bank of the Ogeechee River close to where it empties into the ocean. That means this area contains brackish water which is a mixture of saltwater and freshwater where they meet at the ocean. The best and biggest local shrimp are plentiful here and was what the game wardens had started to cook up for later as part of a low country boil recipe.

Michael was astonished by all the things going on here. After passing the cooking area, they went to an outside presentation area. There was a group gathered sitting on benches in front of a small stage. A uniformed ranger was giving the presentation and was pointing to areas around the park as he spoke. Levi, Michael and Eliza found seats close to the stage and started listening. They could hear the story he was telling dated back to the Civil War. He was presenting to his visitors the story of how Fort McAllister survived being defeated by General Sherman and from the Monitor that was shelling them from the river. From where they sat they could see the mounds of dirt he pointed to during his presentation that were used instead of walls during the Civil War to absorb the impact of cannonfire from confederate ships attacking the fort from the Ogeechee River. In that way, Fort McAllister survived being defeated or even captured during the Civil War.

Another presentation was a demonstration on how the Union soldiers turned railroad ties or rails into what they called bowties or some folks called them neckties. The march of General Sherman's army through Georgia included damaging railroad tracks beyond repair. One way was to remove railroad ties from the tracks, lay the iron rail across a bonfire until the metal became hot enough to soften some, then men would pick up the rail by each end and slam the softened metal middle of the railroad tie around a tree trunk until the ends cross. That's the bowtie. It would be unusable as a railroad track after that.

After the brief description, they saw volunteers standing by who were dressed as Union soldiers and planned to make a real bow tie out of a railroad tie right in front of them. Michael wanted to get as close as he could so the three of them got in the front row. The bonfire was red hot with coals glowing red and the railroad tie was already lying across it heating up. Michael was enjoying feeling the heat of the bonfire too. He had never been this close to a large fire. It soon began turning red and weakening the center. With three volunteers at each end they wrapped blankets around the ends of the hot rails and picked up the tie. They found a nearby tree and began the demonstration by running and yelling as they slammed the middle of the rail into the tree and continued on around as far as it would go before stopping, bending the softened metal around the tree and making the rail worthless for reuse as a railroad track. It was a great demonstration and worked perfectly, a brilliant strategy by General Sherman, to cut off supply lines in the South.

At the end of the presentation while another railroad tie was heating up on the bonfire for another demonstration, the ranger saw Eliza sitting in the audience. He introduced her and she stood up. He informed the audience that Eliza and her friends will be giving a presentation on how they rescued the famous football players and their family from being castaways. A few members of the audience began clapping and a few more joined in. Everyone had heard about this miraculous story.

Levi, Eliza and Michael got up and walked outside to talk until their time came to give their presentation. Levi had a few questions for Michael.

"Michael, what made you abandon the supership?" Levi asked.

"I had to ditch it," he exclaimed bluntly. "No choice," he added as a matter of fact. "The Russians were about to catch me so I abandoned it and made for that island," Levi listened intently.

"Wow, I would never have thought of that. That was great thinking," Eliza said.

"No, not really, that was the only choice I had, just like Daniel Craig in James Bond. I saw it in a movie when James Bond had to ditch his brand new Aston Martin. I figured if he could dump that car I guess I could dump this one." He ended his story with, "Da nana na na da da da na nana na naaa" as he sang the final sequence to the 007 theme song.

He went on to say that the Russians saw him right away but no way could they catch him. "I went deeper and deeper but I couldn't shake them. They had me locked on radar. I could see what they were doing. It looked like they were lining up for a torpedo shot. We were pretty far out and pretty deep, but I guess they decided they better not, so they sent out a spy drone sub instead. I lost control of the supership when I damaged it making evasive maneuvers. I couldn't get back up so I had to abandon her. I came up and at first I thought I was going to have to swim forever but I didn't have to, nope. I saw this little island on the horizon and headed that way."

"I'm sorry it took us so long to find you, Michael," Levi said.

Michael replied, "Are you kidding? It's been great. Until I met you guys, I was afraid you wouldn't like me, you know, because I'm different from you."

"In case you haven't noticed, Michael, we are different from each other too," Eliza said.

"I know, but it's different for me," Michael added. "But this Christmas has been great! I saw my first Christmas boat parade, I chased a Russian sub and then it chased me! Wait...I saw a ghost ship too," Levi's mouth dropped open. He had heard about ghost ships. Seamen have claimed they've been seeing them for centuries. Large sailing ships, like the old and battered ships in the "Pirates of the Caribbean" movies, are totally dark and deserted of live people quietly moving across the ocean. Visual sightings always seemed obscured by fog or darkness but eyewitnesses were certain they saw them and were frightened to death by the sight. They all said that they had to believe what they saw with their own eyes, and they saw them as a bad omen.

"You saw a real ghost ship?" Levi asked.

"Yeah, I heard it first. It was so dark I could barely see but I kept hearing something rowing, like a big ship was closing in on me. When it got close enough to see, I could tell it was heading straight towards me. It was so big and the bow was so high up and it looked a thousand years old," Michael took a breath, "Well, then something even more scary happened."

"What?" asked Levi.

"I went underwater to keep from being spotted. I was under long enough to count to ten and when I came back up," he paused, looked directly at Levi and said, "It was gone."

Levi's mouth was still open, then he asked, "It vanished?"

"Totally," Michael finished.

"Wow, Michael, that's crazy," Eliza said.

"I know," Michael continued, "But then I managed to swim all the way to that little island. It must have been ten miles. That's when I met the greatest man I ever met, named Cap. He taught me everything I needed to know about shrimp boats. I just might be a shrimp boat captain one day."

"Yeah?" Levi asked, "Can I be your first mate?"

"That would be great," Michael said. "We could be like Forrest Gump and Lt. Dan!" They both laughed out loud again. "But that was great thinking of you switching places with me on the boat. I didn't even know you were there until Jay told me. I bet that Coast Guard guy thought he was going crazy."

"Yeah," Levi added, "Cap couldn't believe HIS own eyes when I climbed on board."

"I bet that Coast Guard captain thought he had me this time for sure, but no sweat, Levi. If I can keep from getting captured by a Russian sub, I can play keep away from one small Coast Guard boat." He raised his right hand to receive a high-five smack back from Levi. "I know how to play this cat-and-mouse game of keep away. I can easily stay ahead of him. He has no chance. I'm like Moriarty, I will always stay ahead of the Coast Guard like Moriarty always stayed ahead of Sherlock Holmes," Michael finished. "I really wasn't expecting you to take my place. That was the greatest thing I ever saw."

"Yeah, thanks, and I got to ride on the shrimp boat with Cap. He didn't ever know who you really were, did he?" Levi asked.

"No, I think he has to suspect something now, though," Michael then asked, "Did Cap say anything about me after you went onboard?"

Levi said, "He saw the Coast Guard boat closing in. At first he didn't know what was going on, then he said, you looked like you were getting nervous."

Michael jumped in, "I wasn't getting nervous. I just knew I was going to have to hide somewhere. Then I saw Jay acting crazy beside us."

"Yeah, Cap said when you saw the super ship on one side and the Coast Guard ship on the other side of you, he said you told him thanks for everything but you had to go home now, that your family had found you."

"I said that," Michael confirmed.

Then Levi said, "That's when I told him I was your cousin and that your mother was worried about you."

There was a pause, and then Michael smiled and exclaimed, "She was, too! She hugged me so hard she nearly pinched my head off!" They both laughed out loud.

Michael looked around the park at the many Live Oak trees scattered among the palm trees. They were draped with heavy, gray moss clinging to their branches over thin green leaves that turned brown on the ground. Thick, long, low limbs of the great oaks, some a hundred years old, extended out from enormous trunks, bending and curving to the ground and back up to finally tapering to fine tips all showing signs of new growth. These decades' old limbs were formed and bent by years of harsh weather, strong and sustained winds, even hurricane force winds at times over the decades helped to shape these strong limbs. Michael thought they were beautiful during the daylight but thought the crooked limbs looked kind of eerie at night. Some of the limbs were over thirty feet long and there wasn't just one of these magnificent trees around here, they were everywhere.

"It's really beautiful with these trees and all," Michael said.

"Yeah, I guess so," Levi agreed, looking around.

"But do you know where I'd really like to go?" Michael asked Levi.

"No, where?" Levi asked.

"Disney World!" Michael said, smiling big.

"Yeah, it's great," said Levi, who had been to Disney World in Florida. "Maybe the next time we go, you could go with us," Levi suggested.

"That'd be awesome," Michael said.

"Hey, let's go watch the soldiers again!" Levi said suddenly at Michael.

"Okay," Michael said as they jumped up, "I can't believe I just saw Civil War soldiers make a bow tie out of a railroad rail like General Sherman ordered his men to do to stop the trains from supplying the South. It's like we're going back in time. This is great!" Michael exclaimed.

"Okay, and then let's go see what's inside the museum before we set up for our presentation!" Eliza exclaimed.

The three of them took off.

Back in Charleston, Brad Reno wanted to talk to his lifelong friend, Capt. Jack, aka Cap, to his friends. He knew from past years that he should be back by now from fishing in warmer waters over the last few months. He knew Cap didn't use cell phones so he made the trek down to the docks to see if his old friend had returned from the Bahamas where he took his boat to catch shrimp over the winter. He brought a bottle of Jack Daniels to his old friend to welcome him back to Charleston.

He saw the boat as soon as he parked and could hear the old sailor talking as he walked toward the shrimp boat. He recognized his voice. It was coarse and loud and reached him clearly across the water. It was a voice Brad had heard as a kid growing up here. He remembered how Cap would become aggravated in his voice but his hands were steady. Now he was mumbling and complaining at a screw he was trying to loosen, Brad started smiling. He saw him down there taking things apart and cleaning parts as he approached the moored boat. Cap looked up.

"Well, Brad Reno, come on board you old seadog, you," Cap called to his old friend.

"It's good to see you Cap. I've been wondering how it's been going!" Brad asked, grinning back.

"Good! Good! Brad, my boy. Come aboard. I had quite a good season; how about with you?"

"That's what I wanted to talk to you about. I needed you with me last week."

"Is that right?" Cap inquired, and Brad began telling this fantastical story about this encounter with a giant, a one hundred foot long colossal squid, with eight arms and two tentacles over fifty feet long. He handed Cap the brown paper bag.

"That sounds like a great fish tale. I think I'd like to hear that one," and nodded his head. "Come on board. I've got a story for you," Cap offered up to Brad.

"Oh yeah?" Brad asked back.

"Yep, as a matter of fact I met a young man that reminded me of you when you were a kid. His name is Michael. Oh, and I think I may have seen a UFO," he finished.

"Okay, you first," Cap said.

Brad sat down on a built-in storage box full of extra netting. "Do you remember how the last time I was here we were talking about that giant squid?"

"Yes, Wuss, that treacherous man-eater," Cap mumbled under his breath as he opened the bottle. Brad started his story and Cap brought out two cups from his galley.

"Well, Cap, in Japan..."

"Japan!" Cap responded.

"Yeah, okay," Brad said, "Let me fill the story in a little. I was sitting quietly at home, minding my own business, when I got an email from this reporter, Crystal Brook, from St. Petersburg. She was the one who did the newspaper story on Wuss. Anyway she wanted me to go to San Diego with her to talk about Wuss to a bunch of scientists. Apparently, like I was saying last time, we haven't ever seen a colossal squid in this part of the ocean but over there in California, they have a problem and Japan has a problem. There's still a lot that needs to be learned about these things like their behavior for one. In California they have a different kind of squid. They have one there off the coast called Humboldts. These get up to seven feet long and they have really messed up fishing there. A lot of the fishermen have had to move to other areas entirely. Anyway, they invited Crystal and extended the invitation to me in hopes that I might contribute something useful to their limited bank of knowledge on these things."

Cap handed Brad a coffee cup with about two shots of Jack Daniels and a paper cup of water to put out the fire. Brad accepted the drinks. "Thanks," he said and continued, "While I was standing right there on board a research boat, a call from Japan came in for this scientist I was talking to, from a Japanese university. Crystal is also standing close by and hears the whole story. It seems there was another colossal squid spotted off the coast of Japan in the area of that nuclear power accident they had there in 2011. A colossal squid had inhabited radiated waters and had made a home there. It measured over one hundred feet long." He stopped, took a sip of the Tennessee Whiskey and washed it down with a little water.

"A hundred feet long huh?" Cap asked. "Sounds like a mighty tall tale."

Brad laughed, "It was crazy, but that wasn't the worst part."

"What was the worst part?" Cap asked.

"The worst part, you mean other than a giant squid a hundred feet long? Okay, I'll tell you, Cap, one that can have hundreds of babies. I think we are going to see these again. These, though, won't have to be tagged; we'll be able to identify these with Geiger counters because these baby chicks are all radioactive."

Cap listened without cracking a smile taking in the seriousness in Brad's voice. "That's what I wanted to talk to you about. I don't know if it's something we should be concerned with or not. I mean, if these squids go back to deep water where they belong then they may never be seen again. The entire species can return to the realm of myths and legends."

"Aye," Cap started, "There's a lot of water between here and Japan."

"That's true but the population of these giants are about to explode," Brad said.

Cap looked at him more seriously and said, "Thanks for the warning. I'll keep my eye out. I already seen things out there I didn't know existed. Seeing one of those would at least be something I could explain." The two men clicked their cups together and each took a sip of the whiskey. Brad took a sip of water as his eyes began to water.

Looking out across the water with his friend, Brad saw the sun was creating a beautiful evening. He continued, "There's a lot that scares me about these things. They're smart like dogs from what I've learned and experienced first-hand. I'm convinced they are not likely something you want to put in your fish tank."

Brad wanted to get this off his chest, "There's nothing you can compare them to that walks around out of the water, nothing close to a 100 feet tall, not a grizzly bear or anything. If you spotted one of these, he would likely look like a giant spider 100 feet tall, with two long tapering tentacles fifty feet long each and fluid arms with suction cups as big as your head armed with sharp teeth that can reach out, explore tight areas to find and then grab food, bring it to its mouth and eat immediately. None of this, I'll store you in a web for later nonsense. This type of creature is a hunter/predator and is not afraid to go hunting. They don't need to store food because food is readily available to them. They're like undisciplined juveniles with voracious appetites and the entire ocean is their buffet. They eat what they want to eat and they aren't picky."

Cap reached for the whiskey bottle and poured himself another drink before offering Brad another. Brad was getting worked up so he handed Cap his cup. Cap poured another shot into the cup and handed it back to Brad. He took a breath and accepted the drink back before continuing this part of his tale.

"Getting back to this squid," he looked at Cap. "I've had time to think about this but if you're within a hundred feet of him and you can't close off yourself in a room or big box, then you are his next meal because you are not going to out swim him. These squid are quiet and they can fly underwater. Plus, they can see exponentially better than you because they have huge eyes." He took another little sip of his drink and this time refrained from drinking the water.

"Imagine a lot of these giant squids, 100 feet long from the top of the body to the end of a tentacle. Now, and here's the biggest kicker, in deep dark water they are so quiet and well camouflaged, you can't even see them when you are right next to them. That's what we have here Cap. A perfect predator like in the Danny Glover movie where predators come from another planet to hunt people for sport but it's not really a sport is it, because the people can't see them. That's the way it is with these things. If you are swimming around in their environment, which is really anywhere now from the surface to miles deep in pitch black darkness, these 100 foot long monsters can see you but you can't see them. They have enormous eyes and it's not just for seeing distance, its enormous size allows it to see in virtual darkness. Its retina catches even the smallest amount of light and that allows these things to see in near total blackness. That means that they can see you but you can't see them. That's quite an advantage, don't you think? And to be honest with you I don't think I want to ever see one of things coming after me while I'm in the water again."

"Aye," Cap agreed, "I've never seen one of these devils and I pray I never do." The two men sat there quietly for a moment.

"What's your story, Cap?" Brad asked as he pondered the monsters in his head.

"Oh, it's not a fishing story, Brad; it's a story of a little boy, named Michael." So he began, "I was sitting out on the deck one evening and I saw something stirring the water far out that caught the reflection of the moon and I started watching it. I wasn't sure what it was but it kept coming in my direction. At first I thought it was a manatee or maybe a small whale that had gotten separated from its pod but it never went underwater. It just swam, dogpaddle style, all the way in. It came up to the dock and climbed the ladder. That's when I saw it was a boy, about elevenish. He didn't look like any other boy I'd ever seen, Brad. His skin was white. I mean white, not just pale. His head was shaped a little differently too but he spoke perfect English and even worked on my boat for a while."

Brad was mesmerized now. He wanted to hear this story. "Who was he?" Brad asked.

"Well, now that's the strange part, isn't it? I don't know who he was but I know who he wasn't. He wasn't human," he finished. Brad looked at Cap like he said he just saw a pink elephant.

"What was he if he wasn't human?" Brad asked, smiling now.

"I think he was an alien," Cap said. "I saw him jump into the water in the middle of the ocean after a small fast sub approached my boat underwater, another boy climbed out of the water, a normal looking boy and changed places with him, but Michael left along with the sub."

Brad didn't know what to say. "That's strange. Who was the boy who climbed into your boat?"

"His name was Levi and he rode with me part of the way back. Later after the Coast Guard went away..."

"The Coast Guard?" Brad asked.

"Yes, it was strange. Anyway after they went away the sub came back, the boys said bye, jumped in the water and I never saw either them or the sub anymore," Cap concluded his story.

"But if Michael was an alien, how could he speak English as well as you say?" Brad asked.

"I don't know. I hadn't figured that part out yet," Cap answered.

"Who was the other boy?" Brad asked next.

"Levi?" he asked. "I didn't ask," Cap answered.

"Great story Cap," Brad said

"Yours too," Cap conceded.

Each man pondered the other man's story. Then Brad asked the old fisherman, "Whose story do you think is easier to believe? That I saw a 100 foot long sea monster or that you saw aliens?"

"You got a point. We both sound crazy," said Cap. "I ain't telling anybody," he said as he raised his cup.

"I'll drink to that," Brad agreed, as they clinked their cups together.

The End

Art Designer: Eden Pethel